The Factory Witches of Lowell

The Factory
Witches of Lowell

C. S. Malerich

A TOM DOHERTY ASSOCIATES BOOK

NEW YORK

This is a work of fiction. All of the characters, organizations, and events portrayed in this novella are either products of the author's imagination or are used fictitiously.

THE FACTORY WITCHES OF LOWELL

Copyright © 2020 by C. S. Malerich

Cover design by Jaya Miceli
Cover photographs: red string © Shutterstock.com;
tangled thread © Getty Images

Edited by Carl Engle-Laird

A Tordotcom Book
Published by Tom Doherty Associates
120 Broadway
New York, NY 10271

www.tor.com

Tor® is a registered trademark of
Macmillan Publishing Group, LLC.

ISBN 978-1-250-75655-8 (ebook)
ISBN 978-1-250-75656-5 (trade paperback)

First Edition: November 2020

The Factory Witches of Lowell

1

The Foot Loom

THE EIGHTH OF APRIL found the Merrimack River running sure and fast with thawing snows, which set the wheels of the cotton mills turning again after the freeze of last month; the agent Mr. Boott devoted his entire evening's correspondence to sharing this felicitous news. The Boston gentlemen whom he addressed had built the industrial city of Lowell, not with their hands but with more mystical faculties like "ingenuity" and "entrepreneurship." And money, of course. Most mystical of all.

Textile production, the agent wrote, now proceeded at a pace to match last November's. With the minor adjustment to the mill girls' rent, the owners could expect returns of twenty-two percent again by mid-August. Mr. Boott signed the final letter with a confident flourish of his pen, extinguished the lamps in his study, and retired.

~

As this God-fearing man greeted his bed, the young women of Mrs. Hanson's boardinghouse were leaving theirs. Groping along the banister or holding fast to the girl in front of them, they deserted the dormitories and climbed to the attic, where the taller among them had to stoop to avoid knocking skulls against the eaves.

Creaks and cracks on the staircase, and the susurration of whispers up and down, would have surely roused the house's matron from her own bed on the first floor, had she not been awake since supper. Indeed, Mrs. Hanson herself had progressed to the attic an hour before, where she took up a stool in the corner, while two of the mill girls, Judith Whittier and Hannah Pickering, made preparations.

"Have you any siblings living?" asked Hannah, as she sliced a lock of coppery curls from her head, then dropped it into the collection that lay before Mrs. Hanson's ancient spinning wheel.

"Yes, four. One brother. Three sisters," said Judith, the shorter and sturdier of the two. The pile already contained a lock of her own brown hair, as well as blacks and blonds, in every texture from pin-straight and fine to tightly coiled curls. "*True.* And you, your siblings?"

"None living. Five dead in childhood, one brother lost at sea." Hannah's voice was as thin and reedy as she was, weak from frequent coughing. "True!" she announced, after clearing her phlegmatic throat.

"Try something harder," Mrs. Hanson suggested, as the two girls set to spinning the motley locks into thread. "Something you've reason to lie about."

"Very well." Judith sniffed as she set the wheel spinning with her palm. She would have preferred to leave the matron out of it entirely, but Hannah had said they must have Mrs. Hanson's permission if they meant to use her wheel and loom, and she was sure to scent out any mischief in the house.

Fortunately, this seemed to be the sort of mischief Mrs. Hanson liked.

"Why did you leave Dover?" Hannah asked.

"Half the girls there promised never to strike again," Judith replied. "I wouldn't take that pledge. And no corporation for miles would hire me."

This history came as no surprise to the matron. Judith resembled an animal bred to fight, like a mastiff or bulldog, and her character so far only matched her countenance.

"True," she admitted. "My turn: are you a witch, Hannah Pickering?"

From the way her narrow shoulders stiffened, Judith knew Hannah disliked the question. Which Judith regretted, but which also made it useful for their purpose.

"I have always had an unusual gift," Hannah answered,

speaking to the spindle. "But I haven't made a spell before today."

Judith nodded, even before Hannah pronounced her words truthful.

"I have one," said Mrs. Hanson. "Judith Whittier, who are you in love with?"

Judith scowled and shook the loose hair that hung down her back. "Who says I'm in love with anyone?"

"She's only bound to tell *me* the truth, Mrs. H. To you, she can lie as much as she likes."

"Then you ask her," replied the matron, saucy as any of her young charges.

But the attic was filling with more girls. From the dormitory where Judith and Hannah slept also came Lucy, who was flaxen-haired and sunny whether it was midnight or not, singing "Barbara Allen." Beside her, Lydia bore herself stiffly and with great dignity, her rosebud lips pursed. Because Lucy worked as a "drawing-in" girl in the factories, stringing the looms, and Lydia had a deft hand despite her disposition, Judith set them to threading the harnesses of the foot loom in the center of the attic. Meanwhile, Georgie Hempstead took over spinning from Hannah, and Abigail North—tiniest of the boarders in Mrs. Hanson's house but two years senior to Judith—wound bobbins.

As their labors continued and more girls joined in, Judith thanked Mrs. Hanson for the loan of her stool, set it before the loom, and climbed atop. "My sisters," she addressed them, "to make our stand against the greed of our employers is of course noble and just." Her voice carried through the attic as well as any preacher's, whether Methodist, Unitarian, or Universalist, and inspired nods of agreement and exclamations of "Amen!" just the same. "But as you may know—as you know now—I was in Dover before Lowell, where the mill owners are not so enlightened even as here. We struck. We lost."

The attic grew quiet. The only sound was the scraping of chalk against the floorboards as Hannah drew a circle around the loom. Crowded though it was, any girl not engaged in some task drew her feet beyond this ring, as surely as if it marked a picket of bristling bayonets.

"We were crushed," said Judith, "for lack of resolution more than lack of numbers. A strike is nothing if a worker may pledge herself to it today and return to the factory tomorrow. So we gather here, tonight, to unite and entwine our fate." Around her she could count thirty-one weavers and spinners, elbow-to-elbow below the eaves. "Emelie and Sarah have already left—"

"I'm here," protested Sarah Payne, from among the press of operatives.

"So am I," called Sarah Hemingway.

"Sarah *Adams* and Emelie have already left—"

"Only until we're back at work," said Lucy, from Judith's right.

"Some of us," Lydia sniffed, "have families to think of." She touched the shorn patch of scalp on her own head regretfully. *Yes, yes,* thought Judith, impatient: Lydia had beautiful hair, sable dark; under other circumstances, it would have been a crime to damage it, but—

Her chalk circle complete, Hannah pressed close behind Judith, and Judith steadied herself atop the stool by reaching for the taller girl's shoulder. This assembly of mill operatives would listen to her if she spoke with assurance. "When we strike, we *are* thinking of our families. All of us are sisters of the mills, or we soon will be."

Lydia had not finished. "And you're sure this—kitchen magic will do the job?"

"Kitchen magic has its uses," Mrs. Hanson called from the corner.

Others spoke up in agreement. Every one knew a country wife who twisted charms for a child's health or a sweetheart's loyalty, and not a few had swallowed Mrs. Hanson's tonics. Judith looked at Hannah, wondering if she would add her voice. Only someone with the Sight could say if the charm truly made the difference.

"These aren't the Dark Ages," Lucy coaxed Lydia. "There's no Witchfinder General to come after us."

"But Mr. Boott is sure to."

"Hannah," Judith urged softly, hoping her word might put an end to debate.

Instead, Hannah had a coughing fit. Judith passed her a handkerchief, and when she had done and wiped her mouth clean, she turned toward Lydia. "It will work," she said. Though her voice was strained, her pale face had an authority that surpassed schoolmasters, overseers, and most clergymen. "I have Seen it."

"Oh, you claim to know the future now?"

"No. But I know your soul."

In spite of herself, Lydia gave a little shudder. She truly was the model of the mills, Judith reflected: with a little money in her pocket and a little leisure at the end of her days, she had become the belle of Lowell, coiffed, ribboned, and rational. She was the very sort of girl Mr. Boott and the Boston gentlemen would parade before capitalists and working men alike, as if to say: *Behold! Modern industry shall set your daughters free!*

They'd soon see how much freedom an industrious woman might claim.

Judith climbed down from the stool, offering it to Hannah, but the ginger-haired girl remained on the floor as she spoke to the ring of operatives surrounding the loom. "I've been in Lowell as long as anyone, and I know all of you. When we make our pledge tonight, we weave ourselves together as surely as our wages and our board.

Once we act, we *can't* turn our backs on one another."

This time, as all the girls in the attic grew quiet, the shudder went through Judith as well.

In the corner, Mrs. Hanson shook her head. "A true Seer. I never thought I'd meet one in my life. If I had her gift, lambs, I'd be living in London or Paris, nice as a queen."

At that, Georgie piped up. "We'd miss you so, Mrs. H!"

"Not her cooking," said Sarah Payne.

Laughter having brought the girls together to one mind again, Lucy took Hannah's directions and began lighting five candles at the five points marked on the chalk circle.

Unassuaged, Lydia slid close to Judith. "We don't know what will happen," she hissed. "No one's done this before."

"She has," said Judith. "This very night."

Lydia's rosebud mouth became a tiny O.

"While the rest of you were washing up supper, we pledged, she and I, never to lie to one another, and it worked." Judith showed Lydia where she'd tied the thin braid of dark brown and copper-colored hair—hers and Hannah's—around her pinky finger.

At last, "We're ready," said Lucy, gesturing to the loom grandly, as if she were revealing it to them for the first time. Within the five candles' glow, now the assembled workers could appreciate the motley hair-spun threads that were strung through the harnesses.

"Everyone," Hannah called, suppressing a cough, "keep your hair loose and your arms uncrossed. No one must leave this room until it's done. Lydia, why don't you begin it?"

Lydia's mouth opened again in surprise, but she stepped forward, taking the shuttle and a bobbin from Hannah. In the motion all the weavers knew well, she tucked the thread into one end of the corn husk–shaped shuttle, and raised the other end to her lips to suck it through.

She sighed like a swooning heroine. "The only man I'm allowed to kiss!"

All the girls shared a gallows laugh. In the mills they called it "The Kiss of Death" because each time, they must suck some cotton lint into their lungs along with the thread. If the whale-oil smoke and cotton dust didn't give them a cough like Hannah's, enough kisses would.

Lydia was already placing one foot on the pedal. "Like this?" she asked. With Lydia's foot pressing down, one harness popped up, raising half the warp threads, leaving a gap to pass the shuttle through.

"That's it," said Mrs. Hanson. "Keep going."

With more confidence, Lydia pressed her foot up and down, and the loom's gears turned. The harnesses went up-down, up-down, pulling the warp in a familiar dance, while the weaver passed the shuttle to and fro. The operation was not so lightning-fast as the power looms inside the mills, nor so thunderously loud without a hundred others going at the same time, yet the sound and the rhythm felt the same—the music no mill girl could keep from following her home, thrumming through her dreams and all her waking hours. *Ka-thunk ka-thunk ka-thunk.*

Against its accompaniment, Judith waited for Hannah to speak the spell. But Hannah shook her head gently. "You," she said. "My voice won't carry."

Judith sucked her teeth. Very well. She took the page Hannah put in her hands.

> *"Unbound, we come*
> *to bind ourselves.*
> *By hair of head,*
> *we make a vow.*
> *We form this now:*
> *Fact'ry Girls*
> *Union of Lowell.*
> *No work we'll do,*
> *in mill, at loom,*
> *until our demands*
> *are heard and met,*

and sisters agree
our strike's at end."

"Is that it?" Sarah Payne whispered to Mrs. Hanson. "It's not very . . . mystical."

"It doesn't rhyme," remarked Lucy.

"It will do," the matron replied. "Action and intention matter more than poetry."

"*Until our demands are weighed and met,*" Judith repeated, raising her voice to be heard over the crashing loom. "To wit"—she raised the copy Lucy had written out over supper—"there shall be no increase in the cost of boardinghouses without commensurate increase in the wages of the operatives."

The girls cheered, as Judith had thought they might. This was the fresh wound—an extra quarter that would disappear at week's end, allegedly to pay for the costs of their board. While other boardinghouse keepers were more circumspect, Mrs. Hanson confirmed that no part of the twenty-five cents would see the matrons' pockets but instead set out for Boston posthaste.

Around the room, Judith saw teeth biting anxious lips, alongside scowls and clenching fists. *Good.* She read on.

"Time must be kept fairly and honestly. Clocks shall be visible and prominently displayed, and no working girl shall be required to give over more than ten hours, out of every twenty-four, in her employment."

"Ten?" asked Sarah Hemingway with a snort. "Why not nine? Why not eight?"

The workers laughed, some loudly and some with faces shamed by the audacity.

"Factory owners must make arrangements for the proper ventilation of work rooms so that"—she glanced at Hannah solemnly—"no operative endangers her health in pursuit of her livelihood, and so shortens her life.

"And lastly"—she smiled, for this part was most delicious—"the wages of females shall be equal to the wages of males, so that no woman shall be obliged to marry solely to maintain her own upkeep."

"Hear, hear!" shouted Lucy. Several of the girls stamped their feet or beat on the floor to show their approval, while Lydia pedaled fast enough to make the shuttle fly. Someone passed a bag of sweets, while four girls gathered near the lone window and lit Egyptian cigarettes.

In the corner, Mrs. Hanson muttered something about the ill habits of youth. But she took the cigarette Sarah Payne offered her.

2

Bedtime

THE CANDLES WERE DRIPPING into the circle by the time the weavers ended their toil. The cloth slipped off the loom like water made fabric, the motley locks of the girls forming a pattern never before seen. Under Judith's direction, Georgie Hempstead and Florry Bright cut and finished it into bands, one for each member of the Factory Girls' Union of Lowell, which they solemnly tied about one another's left arms. Finally, Hannah lit a sage broom, to end the spell-making. Curfew was long since past, but some of the girls went down intent on games in the parlor or walking in the night air, too full of magic to sleep.

Judith and Hannah were last to leave the attic, after scrubbing clear the chalk circle and sweeping up the stray threads of hair. Bells chimed in the factories, announcing half past four: time for the mill workers to leave their dormitories, just as the pair returned to theirs.

The room welcomed them, warm and snug. Three

beds filled one wall, close enough that a restless sleeper might roll from one mattress to the next without ever waking; at this hour, Lucy and Lydia ought to be rising from the bed nearest the door, Sarah Payne poking Florry awake in the next. This morning, all three beds stood empty, un-slept in.

Hannah carried the dust pan to the fireplace in the opposite wall, while Judith sat on the trunk they shared at the foot of their bed. "It's strange," she said. "I feel sore and heavy as any Saturday after a full week's work. But my heart is thundering like a loom. If you asked me, I could run all the way to Boston!"

"That's the spell working," said Hannah, as she stoked the fire. When the embers glowed, she emptied the pan and watched the strands of her fellows' hair turn bright as golden threads of sunshine. It was not unlike the Sight—if she closed her eyes, in the darkness she could find the delicate tendrils of genius that belonged to the souls around her, winding about whatever might be cherished or made by its owner: Lucy's notebook of poems and fancies, hidden (or so the writer thought) below the mattress. Sarah Payne's knitting needles. Lydia's silver comb. The corn husk doll Florry cradled each night.

"Can it be broken, do you think?"

"Any magic can be undone." She turned to find Judith already lying down, on her side. Though Hannah could have claimed one of the vacant beds for her own, instead she took her usual spot next to Judith, facing her so that they mirrored one another across the pillow. The sweet smell of sage and the bitterness of burnt hair filled the narrow space between them. "If Mr. Boott learns the particulars—"

"No girl would tell *him*. But do you think Mrs. Hanson is sure? Ought we have hidden it from her?"

"We couldn't. We needed the loom, and the loom belongs to her."

"We might have gotten to it without her knowing."

Hannah shook her head. "You can't do magic on a thing that doesn't belong to you, not without the owner's say-so. But you heard her." She had to pause to fill her shallow lungs, and when she spoke again, it was Mrs. Hanson's voice that came out. "'If I had your gift, I'd live nice as a queen.'"

Judith chuckled. "We're quite lucky you chose the life of a poor mill girl. Others may have thought up the strike, but it's because of you we'll win."

Phlegm choked her before she could reply, and Hannah had to sit up to cough into the crook of her elbow; Judith rose along with her, thumping her back.

When she finally had her lungs again: "I don't know. We're only thirty in this house."

"Operatives in every mill have already agreed to join,

and more will soon." With every word, Judith seemed more certain.

"Lydia was difficult. Many of the others will be worse—the pious ones, and the skeptical."

"Lydia is *always* difficult. When the others see us marching, we'll have their respect and soon enough their trust."

Hannah marveled anew at the surety. Many times she had closed her eyes to See Judith's soul ablaze, like some fiery star come down from its sphere to set them all alight. And when Hannah crawled beneath the quilts at the end of a working day, her weary joints unbuckled beside the warm solidity of Judith Whittier. "I would have left months and months ago, if you hadn't come to Lowell—" She had to stop once more for coughing. "It mustn't go on, the way that it's going," Hannah finished, resting her head at last against the pillow. The allure of freedom—an income and a chance to better their station—drew girls from all corners of New England to the mills. But every season, they worked longer and faster, had to tend more looms to make the same wages, and to obey heavier rules—they were becoming less free, not more.

"It won't go on," said Judith, using her fingers to comb Hannah's curls out of the way before she settled next to her.

Beyond the boardinghouses, the factories rang five o'clock: the working day had begun! Hannah felt a thrill of power in her own belly, for once, to ignore their summons, while her co-conspirator spat in triumph at the rafters.

"Our grandfathers didn't shed blood at Bunker Hill so we could be slaves to a *bell*!"

Unwitting, Judith's words conjured a memory in Hannah.

"Are you well?" Judith asked, for she must have felt the Seer go stiff as a plank.

"No. I am remembering..." The vision danced in Hannah's mind's eye—a creature of wings and teeth and scales—coiling about a man's shoulders as he stood upon the auction block. The much-younger Hannah of the memory screamed and wept, as each blink showed her the demon worming its way into the poor soul's chest, suckling at his heart's blood.

Between them, Judith's pinky, ringed in their plaited hair, hooked Hannah's matching finger. "Can you tell me what's wrong?"

"I can but—" Their spellcraft would not suffer Hannah to lie to Judith; if the other girl demanded to know, she must tell.

"You do not want to?"

"No," said Hannah, limbs softening with relief. "I'd

much rather forget that vision than describe it." She rolled to her side, breaking the momentary link of their fingers. "Anyhow"—she resolved to turn distress into jesting—"you never said who you are in love with."

Judith gasped and snatched the coverlet all to herself. "You witch! NO ONE!"

3

The Boott Palace

MR. BOOTT'S HOUSE STOOD in the center of Lowell. The façade was tall and broad, with a porch of Ionic columns in the style of the ancient Greeks, lawns and gardens spread out like palace grounds.

And why oughtn't Kirk Boott have a home as stately as his employers' in Boston? He embodied their authority in Lowell, carrying their orders to every person from the overseers to the youngest bobbin girl. The wishes of the Boston gentlemen would have no meaning whatsoever, except that Mr. Boott, from his starched collar to the golden buckles on his shoes, to his *indeed* palatial home, conveyed the owners' tangible wealth and power.

Moreover, Mr. Boott was a godly man, who cared for the town and its mills and its young female operatives as much as any pastor for his flock. He'd provided promenades and parks for their amusement, clean homes for their safety, and firm rules and regulations for the care of their souls. What other factory posted exhortations against drinking and gambling? Which other employer not only provided beds to his workers but told them clearly when to be in (and out of) those beds? What other town could boast five thousand unmarried young women and not one case of bastardry?

Yet here in his library sat another overseer, telling another tale of mutiny.

"Third day in a row," said Mr. Curtis, overseer of the Merrimack Corporation. "Third in a row they do not come!" His was a thin face, somewhat overly endowed with crooked nose, that did nothing to hide his tempers.

"Certainly it isn't every girl," said Mr. Boott, hoping a calm demeanor might prevent his visitor from upsetting the tea service.

"Today I have enough weavers for one floor only! And not enough spinners to keep them in thread."

Mr. Boott noted as much in his ledger. "They can't stay out forever. They require wages for their room and board."

Curtis's singular nostrils flared. "You don't know women, do you? They'll last for weeks on spite alone." He slapped the desk like an impertinent schoolboy, which caused Mr. Boott's pen to splutter.

A frown creased the agent's face. With his powers of empathy, it was no great exertion to imagine many a man (or woman) chafed under Curtis's supervision. "Let it not be said we are cruel masters," he said, coming to a decision. "Give the operatives who've stayed on an extra nickel this week. I'll put it out that any who return at once will get the same."

The overseer scowled. "Better to drag the rebels back in by their hair."

"To what purpose?" Mr. Boott blotted his ledger. "Earning even more spite?"

"At least you ought to make an example of the ringleaders. I could point to a few."

"I am sure you could. But this isn't the old world, and our operatives aren't serfs to be whipped and transported."

The maid interrupted to announce visitors at the front door. None too disappointed to leave this meeting, Mr. Boott rose to go and see. A dozen mill girls were standing between the Greek columns.

"Mr. Boott, we are so pleased to find you at home," said a short, sturdy child of fifteen or sixteen.

"Good morning." Something about the girls' appearance disquieted Mr. Boott, beyond the obvious fact that they were on his porch instead of in the factories. "Who might I have the honor of addressing?" His first glance had been wrong: there were more than a dozen of them. Many more.

The one who had spoken smiled. "We represent the

Factory Girls' Union of Lowell."

Union? So it was war, was it? The working men—women—against the capitalists; precisely the sort of thing he and his employers had designed Lowell to prevent.

Mr. Boott cleared his throat and chose to remain calm. "Oh? What's your business with me?" It would not be the owners' side that opened hostilities.

"You may have noticed that we have not returned to work since Friday. We are here to present you with our demands before we do so."

Before he understood what was happening, she had pressed a leaf of paper into his hand. Mr. Boott was literate—quite so—and yet his mind could not make meaning of the runes it found on that page. At most, it snatched out words he recognized. *Clocks . . . boarding-houses . . . ventilation . . . health . . . females . . . equal.*

"None of us," said the girl who had handed him the page, "will return to our posts until the corporations comply with these demands in good faith."

Mr. Boott stared, wondering what sort of creature he was facing. Not a lovely one to look at: her small eyes were black and round, and quashed together with a blunt nose at the central latitude of her face. A bonnet might have helped, but her head was bare, brown hair wild. Indeed, all the young female faces before him were framed with free-flowing locks, from the freckle-faced girl with flaxen hair to the dusky beauty with lips like a gem. Each one wore an armband of the most curious variegated cloth. It wasn't cotton.

The skin at the back of Mr. Boott's neck prickled.

"My dear young woman," he began, composing his features carefully into a smile. "Young *women*," he added, acknowledging the full crowd. "Clearly, you have considered your lot and noticed many arenas for improvement. I understand. But even the simplest of alterations cannot be accomplished in the space of a day."

The black-eyed leader cocked her head. "We'll wait."

Kirk Boott, of course, was a Christian and an educated man—a man in full mastery of his base animal nature. And yet, when she held her face at that angle, every bit of him, from the marrow of his bones to the tip of his eyelashes, wanted nothing more than to shatter that arrogant smirk against the back of his hand.

Instead, he swallowed and patiently, as if speaking to his own adorable but wayward progeny, explained to the young women that they worked for a modern concern, a species which required continuous production to survive among its rivals. "I promise you," he finally said, "the Boston gentlemen will get a full account of your demands. But no change will be possible unless you return to work. Any girl"—he redoubled his tolerant smile—"who does so immediately will receive an additional nickel in her pocket at the end of the week."

That quieted the little swarm.

"A nickel?" asked the stout little leader.

"Yes," he replied, pleased that he had chosen this gentle, generous form of persuasion. "This week, and next, until the end of your contracts."

"You raised our board by twenty-five cents last week."

Mr. Boott's mouth opened but he had no reply.

The girl shook her head. "We are a union now. Tell your masters." She nodded at the paper in his hands and then gave some signal to her sisters. The crowd turned about and marched away, militaristic precision in their steps.

Mr. Boott shut the door before they were out of sight. He stretched out an arm to the lintel, supporting himself while his limbs took to trembling.

"Well, did the carrot move the mules?"

Mr. Boott lifted his head. Curtis stood watching him, those prodigious nostrils flaring with the answer he must already know.

"This impertinence is uncanny."

"That's what comes of giving women a free rein. Wages spoil them—soon as they have money in hand, they get to think they're people-in-the-world and they want to say what's so. I've seen it even in some men. Better ship this lot back to the farms and let your Boston nabobs start over."

Mr. Boott grimaced, remembering who was the superior man. Curtis was a blunt instrument—useful in the appropriate moment but hopeless in most others. Instead of listening to the overseer further, Mr. Boott thought about the bands of strange cloth wound about the girls' arms, and their hair flowing wild over their shoulders. He thought of the violent temptation that had reared up inside him, to strike their leader.

Might that not be his soul rebelling against the presence of something foul and evil?

Mr. Boott crossed himself, and then thought better of it. Witchcraft? No. There hadn't been a witch in New England for two hundred years. Besides, what worker would go so far? This wasn't Lancashire; this was Massachusetts. And yet . . .

These girls were so very defiant.

Mr. Boott crossed himself again.

4

The Advertisement

WORD OF THE BATTLE at the Boott Palace spread from boardinghouse to boardinghouse and from factory to factory, whispered from one worker to another. So too went word of the Union's demands. At all hours, a knock might come at Mrs. Hanson's door, to reveal another girl on the step, her cheeks pink with excitement.

"I'm looking for the Factory Girls' Union," she would say, as if the words themselves were an incantation, and she would be invited inside by Lucy or Georgie or Sarah Hemingway, whichever might be on guard duty. A girl might come eagerly with her hair undone, carrying fistfuls more from the operatives in her weaving room. Or she might arrive skeptically, and then Judith was summoned, always with Hannah, who watched silently through closed eyes while Judith explained that the Union was both a cover of hardiest sailcloth and flimsiest gauze.

"We are the thread, all of us together," Judith said. "If

one of us snaps, the whole bolt might unravel. If we hold fast, the corporations have nothing but empty factories."

If the girl nodded and agreed—and if Hannah did the same—then the house woke again, rose to the attic like the steam off Mrs. Hanson's cook pots, and wove once more, drawing new threads into the Factory Girls' Union of Lowell.

By week's end, there were fewer weavers inside the mills than out. Though many had not yet pledged to the Union, only the least liked and most craven operatives answered the mill bells' call at half past four, and when they did, and the overseers counted their numbers, they only sent them away to the dormitories again. The machines could not run with so few.

~

On the twelfth day of the strike, Florry arrived just in time for supper, to make her daily report. "The men in the Concord Mills are still with us." She had volunteered herself ambassador because she had ten brothers, and knew how to speak so a man would hear.

"That's a piece of luck," Lydia marveled. While the Factory Girls' Union stayed out, the male hands and dyers had no work either.

"It isn't luck, it's Florry's eloquence and the men's

good sense to listen," said Judith.

"Here, come and get it!" Mrs. Hanson bellowed from the end of the long trestle table, as she let a steaming pot clatter onto the surface.

"Gruel again?" asked Sarah Payne, peering inside with disappointment.

"How else can I keep feeding you? Not to mention myself . . ."

"We're only grateful, Mrs. H," said Lucy, wrapping her arms about the matron and forcing a kiss on her cheek. "Girls, think! We could all be homeless by now." The mill owners had stopped payments to the boardinghouse keepers, and some of the matrons had taken retribution against their charges, locking out tenants and tossing their belongings into the street.

"Humph," grunted Mrs. Hanson as she ladled out supper to the nearest of her charges. "I ought to have given the boot to the whole lot of you."

"There's one Boott in particular I wish you *could* give us," said Judith, taking one bowl for herself and one for Hannah. "I'd hang him by his toes in the root cellar until he turned on his masters."

"Stay clear of him. If he's smart, he already suspects every one of you of consorting with the Devil. How long before you're denounced and arrested?"

"He wants us in the mills," said Judith, sliding away

from the matron, "not in jail." She held the two bowls high to avoid clumsy elbows and wrists.

"A few hangings might convince the rest to go back," Mrs. Hanson called after.

"Hangings?" gasped Sarah Hemingway.

Lucy laughed. "She's only trying to frighten us." If Mrs. Hanson voiced any disagreement, it was lost in the clattering of spoons and the chatter of other boarders.

"What proof could they have?" Judith squeezed past the long queue of girls still awaiting their portion. Hannah sat quietly, closest the parlor door and the staircase, and accepted the bowl Judith passed her across the table. "Unless Mrs. H is planning to testify."

"She wouldn't," said Lucy, who had slid along the opposite wall to sit at Hannah's right. "Too soft-hearted."

"Besides," Judith waved one hand while she dug into her gruel as if it were the finest meal she'd ever eaten, "arresting me wouldn't end the strike. Someone else would take the lead."

"Who did you have in mind?" lovely Lydia wanted to know, claiming the next span of bench beside Judith.

Judith shrugged with her mouth full. "Maybe Amy from the Hamilton Mills, or that Vermont girl Mary Paul. She's clever with a speech."

Lydia scowled across the table at Lucy, who grinned and lifted one shoulder.

"There have been more evictions?" Hannah asked, wheezing.

"Two more houses on Prescott Street," little Abigail North confirmed.

"It won't be for long," said Judith. "The owners must be ready to crack."

"You're their confidante now, are you?" asked Lydia, pursing her rosebud mouth.

"Between the late freeze and the strike, they haven't seen a profit in months," Judith replied, without concern. "What else matters to a capitalist?"

Under the table, Hannah's foot nudged her. "We ought to see to the evicted girls. Whether they need help with their things, or—"

"It's done," said Lydia. "Some found rooms with the Universalists, and the rest have gone to Mrs. Warrington's boardinghouse."

With that settled, each of the young militants turned full attention to her food, tasteless as it was. Mrs. Hanson retired to the kitchen, where she took her tea nightly in relative peace.

As they ate, Laura Cate came around with the post, distributing letters and newspaper subscriptions. Most of the news came from home, as often about the doings of younger siblings and the family cow as about the strike. Georgie Hempstead gasped when she saw inside her letter, then promptly stood up, went to Mrs. Hanson, and deposited several jingling coins in the matron's palm.

"From my people," said Georgie, blushing. "They said it was for the strike."

"How did they manage?" others wanted to know, and "How much?"

Mrs. Hanson's fist tightened around the coins, hiding them from view. But she said to Georgie, "Your family meant this for you. Are you sure?"

"Sure as sure. It's for all of us."

Meanwhile, Abigail was still as a stone, looking just as hard at the letter in her hands. Patience Smith moved to her side to peek over her shoulder, startling Abigail, who placed the letter facedown on the table.

"What is it?" Patience asked.

"My father is ill," said Abigail. "Too ill to plant."

Smelling trouble, Judith had risen from her seat and came up behind the smaller girl, trailing Lydia and Lucy. Judith didn't scruple to lift the letter from the table and read it. "Your mother begs you to send your wages home, or they will starve next winter—Well," she proceeded swiftly from the letter's contents to her own rebuttal, "not to fear, Abigail! No North will starve while the Factory Girls' Union abides. When our demands are met, you'll send twice as much back to your parents."

"They are all alone," Abigail replied, taking back the

letter. "They have no children at home but the babies, and now I can't help them!" Holding herself, her fingers touched the hair-woven band around her arm and she began to cry.

The others drew close, until the small girl was too bundled up in friendship and care to remove the band from her arm if she'd wanted to.

"Judith is right," Patience assured her. "Your parents won't starve. We'll be back at work soon."

"I'll write to my people," Georgie offered. "Perhaps they've got another coin for yours."

Covered in embraces and kind words, at last Abigail nodded. "Yes," she agreed, "you're right. I don't—I mean, I *know* we're in the right. My mother will be proud when she learns what we do here."

Relieved, Judith returned to find a seat beside Hannah. The Seer hadn't moved but sat, eyes closed, with her face turned to the knot of young women surrounding Abigail. Judith pinched her and told her to eat, pulling over what remained of her own portion. Hannah was too thin as it was; it was a wonder she ever had the strength to manage a power-loom at all, to throw the levers and knock the weft thread home after a bobbin change.

To liven the room, someone called for Lucy to do a reading, but instead of an original ode or acrostic, Lucy stood up on the bench and read out an opinion of the strike from the *Boston Herald,* with all the gravity of a schoolmarm, until all her audience laughed to tears: "'The ambition of a woman ought to begin and end in adorning the domestic sphere, not inciting her sex to riot. Governor Everett must call up the militia and prevent a gynecracy in Lowell.'"

"Hah. I should like to see what the militia does when they see who their enemy is," declared Sarah Hemingway.

"Probably lay down their arms and ask Lydia to dance," said Judith, which neither Lydia nor Hannah smiled at. But Lucy chuckled before announcing she would write a rebuttal to the *Herald.*

Sarah Payne found the next page of newsprint far more distressing. Her brown eyes, wide and liquid at the best of times, grew to the size of saucers as she spread the page across the table. "Oh, look here! Do you see?"

Lydia leaned over and read it out in her clear, declaiming voice: "'WANTED: healthy grown girls and women for mill work. Fair wages and clean board. Must be unmarried. Good character. Lowell, Massachusetts.'"

Many of the young operatives grew quiet. A few muttered oaths as they passed the page around the full length of the table.

"Boston is rife with girls who will answer that ad," said Lydia. "Think of the shiploads of Irish, the orphans and widows—"

"—and not one reason they oughtn't make common cause with us against rich men in gilt houses," said Judith, still wiping at her tears of mirth.

"If they don't join us, they could have a job and wages," said Sarah Hemingway, growing gloomy.

Surrounded by her fellow strikers, Judith could feel their uncertainty tugging at her, like a litter of insistent pups at her skirts. After Abigail had come around, she'd hoped they would show a bit of sterner stuff. "Come now! Don't forget your worth. Sarah Payne," she called, "when you came to Lowell, did you know a warp thread from a weft?"

The girl blushed. "No, not at all. My family never had the money for a loom of our own."

"Who showed you how?"

"Why, Georgie did. We started in the same weaving room."

"Now you run five looms yourself. Five! And Lucy, did you work in any factory before this one?"

"No, Judith," Lucy replied, grinning, for she must have seen at once what their ringleader was about. "It was Betsy Thorne and Sylvia who taught me."

"And you've worked as drawing-in girl for twelve months, haven't you? You see?" Other faces besides Lucy's were brightening now, eyes rising from the floorboards and up from the trestle table.

"Us in this room are worth triple and quadruple what the owners get us for," Judith preached, a gospel she could feel their ears eager to hear. "The corporations may try to replace us, but they'll have no one to teach the new girls, and no one to run the machines meanwhile."

"That's true," murmured Sarah Payne.

"Of course it's true!" Judith cried. "This is no time for faint hearts. We are on the cusp of victory!"

"Hear, hear," said Lucy, rapping her spoon against her bowl.

"Mind the crockery," Mrs. Hanson scolded from the kitchen.

"To victory," wheezed Hannah, raising her cup. "To the Factory Girls' Union of Lowell."

Around her, more cups rose and the chorus went up. "To victory! To the Factory Girls' Union of Lowell!" There was nothing but watery coffee in the cups, but tonight, it sufficed.

5

Loyalty

STILL, NO SOUL SLEPT SOUNDLY in Mrs. Hanson's boardinghouse that night, least of all the little general herself. At dawn, Judith whispered her plea to Hannah that the older girl come with her, away from the dormitory, away from the house, where no anxious ears would hear them.

Together they took the path between the blocks of worker tenements leading toward the factories, quite deserted while the strike lasted. Without thousands on thousands of machines thundering along inside the factories and workers chattering to and fro, all Lowell was peaceful as a churchyard.

"Tell me again what it's like: what you do."

The Seer didn't need to ask what Judith meant. "Think how, if you stare long at a candle's flame, the phantom hangs there even if you shut your eyes."

Judith nodded. She liked this: to hear the older girl speak with confidence on a subject she knew well, her voice rough and low like a carpenter's file against supple pine.

"When I know a person," Hannah continued, "I can spy their phantom in everything that's theirs. What they own, and what they make, and what they use. It all becomes a part of them, soul if not body." She paused, and in the silence, Judith answered the unasked question.

"The problem," she began with a sigh, "is, one, we Union girls are pledged to stay out of the mills until our demands are met. Two, Mr. Boott is determined not to meet them. Therefore, three, as soon as he is able, he will have new workers in the factories, more desperate and more docile."

"Then you are worried about the advertisement? About—about replacements?"

"Of course! The looms don't care who tends them."

"But what you said at supper... Our skills? Knowledge? Were you—"

Judith caught the way she spun the braided band of Judith's hair around her finger. "I meant what I said!" She tossed the loose hair that remained attached to her scalp. When Hannah's mouth opened again, she rushed to finish. "But Boott and his masters won't care: they'll sacrifice a few months' productivity on teaching new weavers and spinners, if at the other end they can declare victory over the Union..."

The Seer only continued to twist that woven ring around her finger.

" . . . Unless," said Judith, taking Hannah's hand so the fretting ceased, "we convince the machines to strike with us."

They stopped now and looked up, to find out where their footsteps had led them. The path that gobbled nearly eight precious minutes of meal times on a working day had taken less than three minutes now that it was empty. The Merrimack Mill, the colossus, stood before them, just over the canal: six stories of red brick, long as a village lane, and nearly a village of its own, and yet only one of the eight in Lowell. Warehouses surrounded the mill, where bales of cotton and bolts of finished cloth were stored, and offices, where the clerks and overseers kept accounts. Another morning would have found Judith and Hannah working on the upper stories of the mill itself, minding three and four looms at a time, with a hundred other girls occupied just the same. Downstairs, hundreds more would be carding and cleaning and spinning cotton on the river-powered wheels, and the smallest ones—children of eight or ten—would be filling baskets and swapping empty bobbins for full.

Today, Judith and Hannah crossed the footbridge alone. Only the flat-bottomed skiffs in the canal broke the stillness, bobbing on the ends of their tethers. Each was piled high with burlap-covered cotton, nowhere to move it because the warehouses were already bursting at the seams.

Judith was more interested in the mill gates. "Closed and padlocked, of course," she muttered, though she tried the iron bars to be sure. The hinges whined, but the gate didn't budge but an inch.

"You plan to bewitch the machines, to be part of the strike?" Hannah's voice rasped.

"Why not? If a person's genius is not only in them but in their things."

The Seer frowned. "With the Union now, it's a new pattern. We're all everywhere"—she lifted her arm with its band of hair-cloth—"and I have to look very carefully to find one person. It's like trying to follow one thread in a field of calico."

Judith didn't have the gift, but she'd felt what Hannah was describing: all of the girls together, warp and weft, so tightly woven, no capitalist could pick them apart. "If a thing is full of our genius, it ought to be a simple thing to cast our spell over it, shouldn't it? The wheels and the looms very especially. Thirteen hours a day, six days a week, we tend them, we feed them, we kiss that damn shuttle! They're full of us, aren't they?"

Hannah turned away. "Of course they are, the greedy things."

Judith pressed on, taking the Seer's left hand again and capturing the right as well for good measure, pulling Hannah to face her. "This gate is padlocked, as I can see. But can *you* See any way for us to influence the machines? We used our hair for solidarity and friendship, to weave ourselves together into a union. Is there not some vessel for loyalty, so that the machines refuse the hands of another?"

She stared into the Seer's heart-shaped face, so pale and freckle-less, willing the remarkable girl to conjure a solution. Hand-in-hand, their palms warmed and softened like candle wax, and a strange bubble of feeling rose from the pit of Judith's stomach.

Hannah's cheeks turned pink and she laughed—suddenly and loudly—and shook herself loose once more.

"What is it?"

"Spittle," said Hannah.

"Spittle?"

"Yes. All spells use genius, but the vessel shapes them. Hair is different from bone is different from blood. Shadows even have some genius in them, but only for spells of seeming, strongest near dawn and dusk. At noon and midnight, the truth would be plain.

"But for loyalty . . . Loyalty needs the passions." Once more, Hannah turned that charming shade of pink, this time from the roots of her copper-hued hair down as far as her collar—and farther, Judith presumed. "The deepness of the lover's kiss." Hannah's gaze met Judith's briefly, before cutting away, looking off into the canal.

Judith ignored the bubbling feeling inside herself, aiming instead for the solution which appeared on the horizon. "Of course! If I didn't know better, I would have said Lydia shares your Seer's gift."

"Lydia?"

"She invoked the Kiss of Death when we wove the Union."

"I recall."

"How do we do it, then? There must be a way to reach the machines." Without hesitation, Judith stepped off the edge of the footbridge, onto the slick stones of the canal's headrace, searching the mill's walls for another portal.

"Judith!" Hannah called. "Judith, be careful! What are you looking for?"

With her right hand against the mill wall for balance, Judith walked along the narrow edge, one foot's heel at the toe of the other, following the canal's flow. Though the fortification showed no obvious weak points, just ahead stood the tower-like housing of the mill wheel, its paddles dipping into the water with each turn, then disappearing upward and inside. The aperture there might be enough to admit one short mill operative and her taller, but willowy, companion. Their feet might get wet.

Or they might brain themselves against the housing, catch limbs in the gear works, or snare themselves below the paddles to drown in the canal.

A hand over her own broke Judith's concentration and she nearly slipped. Hannah's grip steadied her.

"Think, Judith: spells are built on metaphor and connections," the Seer told her. "Find a connection to the mill's machinery, even outside the walls, and they'll be influenced inside."

"The water!" Judith grinned. "It gives the machines their spark."

Hannah nodded without returning the smile. "But not for us. We cannot work magic on the looms and spindles."

"But you said! The machines are full of us, *our* genius—"

Hannah shook her head fiercely. "Judith, look at those bales of cotton you see floating there. Whose genius fills those? Whose blood and sweat?"

"Well—"

"If witchcraft is all so simple as you imagine, did you never wonder that the enslaved wretches who pick that cotton don't lay hexes on the whole White race?" Now Hannah's voice rasped with the conviction of an abolitionist, and Judith marveled that she had never heard the Seer speak on the subject before this moment.

"I—I hadn't considered it," she replied, bewildered.

"All magic is mastery and command, isn't it? You have to have a claim to something before you can cast spells over it, even your own self." Next, she pointed at the laden skiffs in the canal. "That cotton is full of men and women, like snow that's been tramped over, with all their tracks on it. But it doesn't do them a lick of good unless they have the ownership."

Judith clicked her tongue. "Which the law of the land won't admit."

Hannah sighed deeply, and began sidling carefully back to the footbridge. "Let's go before someone spots us and we're both in the stocks for trespass."

For the young woman of action, it galled to retreat now, the plan hardly begun, but she could not continue alone.

They came back single file but walked side by side over the bridge, as they had done daily since Judith's arrival in Lowell; although any other morning would have seen their arms entwined, fond friends. In this mood, Judith shrank to touch Hannah at all.

"Is the law of the land so incontrovertible?" she asked instead. "Not even witchcraft can slip its yoke?"

"The law is witchcraft, Judith," Hannah said quietly. "I've Seen auctions. When the captive stands on the block and the auctioneer begins the bidding, it conjures something . . . something that sucks away at a person's soul. At the end, when the master has his slave bought and paid for, he owns them like a mule or a dog." Her shoulders shook.

Judith swallowed, and lengthened her steps, putting herself where Hannah couldn't help but look at her. "It's a terrible wrong," she said, lifting her arm and its hair-woven band, "but that isn't us. We're fortunate to still belong to ourselves. *And* to each other."

Her own words shocked Judith to stillness. Though she meant to say the members of the Factory Girls' Union, all belonging to one body, the words also seemed to mean something particular about the two of them, flowing from that same *mare incognitum* in her belly that Hannah's blushes had found.

"Do we?" Hannah asked, blinking hard, so that Judith suspected she was not trying to See, but to hide angry tears. "So many times, standing in the work room, I've blinked to See my own self leaking away and filling up my looms. It's like watching my very breath sucked away." Her indignation proved too much for her thin form to contain, and she doubled over in a coughing fit.

"Then we take it back!" Judith declared, as she thumped her back.

When she could breathe again, Hannah straightened and shook her head. "It's as I've been saying, Judith, the machines don't belong to us. Nothing in the mills does."

"Why not? They're more ours than some men in Boston who've never laid hand to thread."

"Capitalists have their paper-craft. They may not See it any more than Mrs. Hanson can See the craft in her tonics, but contracts and deeds conjure too. Like the . . . demon . . . at the slave auctions."

"Oh, Hannah, please, won't you at least try to See a way around it? Else why did we start all this?"

The Seer gazed back with a face forlorn, which Judith half-wanted to kiss and half-wanted to slap, as the new-struck wellspring of feeling continued to bubble inside her.

"Hannah," she began instead, "indulge me: do you know why I am so determined? When I first went to school, I knew my arithmetic better than the schoolmaster's son, who was twice as old. When I finished my sums ahead of all the others, Master Hills was sure I had conned the answers somehow. Without waiting for any explanation, he laid his rod right across my hands!"

She was gratified to observe a wince on the older girl's face. "How did you know your sums so well?"

"My oldest brother taught all of us at home. It was our game." Judith touched each knuckle of her finger, remembering how she had learned to count and add. "Ever since that beating, I've hated masters, overseers, bosses—all these men lording it over, thinking they know best, thinking they have the measure of us! I couldn't give up the fight now, even if they flayed me alive."

She waited, to see how this speech would impress and inspire her co-conspirator.

All Hannah replied was "The schoolmaster beat me also." She coughed. "And my parents did."

"Why?" Now it was Judith marveling, for she could hardly imagine Hannah as a mischievous child.

"The reverend told them they must, if I said I saw things that weren't there."

The bubbling spring in Judith's stomach reached her eyes.

"It didn't make me fierce like you," said Hannah. "I only stopped telling anyone what I Saw. And when I could, I left."

Gently, Judith gathered both of the Seer's hands in hers. "All the more reason to make a stand now. This is your home, Hannah. This is your place. Oughtn't it be a place that treats you well?"

The tall girl sighed. "I'll try, Judith. I'll try to See a way to make the looms faithful."

Judith dropped Hannah's hands to clap hers in delight. "That's all I ask!"

6

The Boardinghouse Keeper

QUILL IN HAND, MR. BOOTT considered the woman before him. She must be past sixty—certainly beyond any epoch when youthful humors might have led her astray. A distinguished spider's web of wrinkles bloomed from the corners of eyes and mouth, segmenting her somber—even sour—face. Her gray dress was clean and her hair neatly tucked below the matching bonnet, in much the same costume worn by the other matrons of Lowell.

Nevertheless, here she was, to plead the case of mutiny.

"You've no cause to stop payment to us keepers." Neither the depth of her chair nor the height of Mr. Boott's desk impressed her. "*We* aren't on strike."

"Ah. Mrs.—Hanson, was it? Yes." He'd noted her name and her position in his diary as soon as she arrived. "You must understand, Mrs. Hanson, that my employers cannot make payments out of nothing. With the mills at a standstill—"

"Surely the Lawrences and Appletons of the world have a line of credit when they need it? We're working hard as ever to feed and shelter your operatives. Or do you *want* a thousand girls starving in the city streets?"

"No, no, no, not in the streets." Mr. Boott cleared his throat and fluffed his cravat. "Naturally, some of the overseers rejoiced to hear that a few of the most—troublesome—girls have been evicted, but I hoped, Mrs. Hanson, I hoped that the matrons might exercise a wiser, motherly influence and persuade the young women back to work."

"I'm paid to feed and house them, not to bully them."

"At present, you're not paid for anything." The agent could hardly help showing his impatience when the woman insisted on misunderstanding him.

"Indeed," said the matron, her thin eyebrows disappearing below the peak of her bonnet. "That is the sole and complete substance of my complaint to you today."

"There will be no money until the mills are running again. I regret I cannot satisfy you."

"Then satisfy the Union girls." She placed one hand on either arm of the chair, squaring up. "Give them what they want—it isn't much—and spin your cotton into gold again. What are you searching for, sir?"

Mr. Boott had risen to the capacious bookshelves, where years of records were bound and collected. "Ah.

Here it is: Merrimack Corporation, Number Seven."

The woman blinked at the invocation of her house, and Mr. Boott nodded approvingly to himself. If she insisted on being heard, he would have some questions of his own answered. "Since you object to having any moral influence upon your charges, perhaps you might not object to influencing *me*, on their behalf?"

Now the lady's eyes grew round, as she watched him open the bound records of her lodgers, and turn the pages. "What do you mean?"

"It's quite simple." He returned to his throne behind the desk. "I am inquiring into the character of your boarders, Mrs. Hanson. Shall we proceed alphabetically? Emelie Adams: tell me about her. Is she a good, churchgoing girl? Ever late for curfew, or gone at odd hours?"

The matron's lips became thin and bloodless. "You may skip Emelie." By her tone, she had lost all taste for this interview. "As well as her sister Sarah. Both left Lowell before the strike began."

"Very well," said the agent, determined to press his advantage. "Who's this, then? Elizabeth Bagley. Tell me about her, for surely you know something. A boardinghouse keeper cares as much for the soul as for the body."

"I can't tell you a thing about their souls," the woman

replied. "Only what they eat and where they sleep at night."

If Mr. Boott had begun this exercise with any mirth, it was long since exhausted. "Florinda Bright," he announced. "Laura Cate. Mary Cook," he went on, searching for some reaction. "You must hear them whispering on the staircase or chattering in the parlor. Surely, you can tell which one introduced this infernal Union business into the house. Lucy Larson. Sarah Payne," he said, choosing names at random now, searching for a reaction. "Hannah Pickering."

The woman's gaze fluttered from his own, seeking to rest anywhere else in the room: window ledge, bookcases, pigeonhole cubbies, the geography of his desk from inkwell to silver quill nippers.

"Yes? This one, Hannah? Who is she?"

"If I'm not in your employ, Mr. Boott, I've nothing to tell you."

"If you're not in my employ, Mrs. Hanson, I've nothing to pay you."

The matron huffed and rose to her feet, gathering up her skirts. "The arrogance of great men!" she murmured.

Mr. Boott was quick, rounding the desk in time to catch her arm before she could pass from the room. "Tell me about Hannah Pickering. She's one of the ringleaders, isn't she?"

"She," began the stout woman, stretching upward to her full height (quite equal to the agent's, as it was), "is a sweet, obedient maiden who's worked in Lowell for four summers without so much as a 'boo' to anyone, and mark me, she'll die of weak lungs before she's twenty, no thanks to you or your masters. Now, unless you plan to clap me in irons, sir, unhand my sleeve."

Abashed, Mr. Boott released her and looked at his polished shoes. Perhaps what she said about this single girl was true, but—

"Aid me, Mrs. Hanson. Be my eyes and ears. You cannot be indifferent to the times in which we live: what if we meet the demands of this Union, and then the river fails, or the cotton wilts, or a hundred mills cover Lancashire to turn out cloth on the cheap? Every corporation in Lowell would be ruined, and that would be the undoing of many an enterprise, from Boston to Charleston—merchants, shippers, planters, all—your boarders included. We are a young nation, newly afloat, with the Empire and all its colonies eager to sink us. Do you think the governor or the president can stand by while their captains of industry are led by the nose? The Boston gentlemen have no wish to quarrel with you, no, nor any of the mill girls. But they must be permitted to *lead*."

The speech quite exhausted the agent, and he did not

expect a word of it to convince the matron. While he reached for his desk, gasping, to his surprise the woman reached out. Her hand cupped his well-shaved cheek in a motherly fashion.

"Their existence," she said, "is a quarrel with me and the mill girls. But I shall think on it, Mr. Boott. Good day."

7

Abigail North

JUDITH AND HANNAH did not return to Mrs. Hanson's until after supper, their bellies yawning with hunger. Though they intended to make straight for the kitchen, no sooner had they set foot across the threshold than Patience Smith hastened up from the foot of the staircase where she'd been sitting, rushed to Judith, and seized her hand.

"Thank heavens you're here!" Patience was breathless, her face giving the lie to her name as she tugged Judith inside. Other girls were lining the staircase, leaning over the banister to watch, or seated around the parlor in clusters, heads lifted in attitudes of disturbed conversation. Tonight, there was no evidence of games, no playing cards, no one seated at the pianoforte.

"What's happened?" asked Judith.

"It's Abigail—she—we—you'd better come and see. Perhaps you too," the girl added to Hannah, less certain.

Irritated more than intrigued, intrigued more than

alarmed, Judith allowed herself to be pulled up the staircase, past the others waiting in various states of agitation. The third floor, they found deserted except for Sarah Payne, who stood knitting outside the doorway of the dormitory shared by Patience, Abigail, and four others. The needles clicked and clacked menacingly, as if singing the tale of their sharp points. After recognizing the three new arrivals, Sarah stood aside, allowing them to enter the dormitory. She swiftly retook her post as soon as Hannah had passed.

Inside the bedroom—even smaller and darker than the room where Hannah and Judith slept on the fourth floor—Lucy and Lydia flanked a bundle of quilt and pillow, which was shaking with sobs.

"It's no less than you deserve, you craven little mouse," Lydia excoriated the sobbing bed clothes. "By heaven, Judith was right!"

"What is this?" asked Judith herself.

Leaving others to explain, Patience went to the fireplace, where she stood worrying a hangnail and watching.

"It's Abigail. She feared for her family." With a weary sigh, Lucy sat down on the bed beside the bundle, which squinting Judith could make out was the pitiful shape of a young woman curled up below the quilt, the pillow mashed over her head with two trembling hands. "She tried to go to Mr. Boott."

All pity that Judith was prepared to feel disappeared. The attitude of the operatives downstairs and Sarah Payne's armed vigil at the door grew clearer. "To Mr. Boott? Why?"

In response, the bundle wailed, and from the fireplace Patience pled her fellow's case. "Judith, don't be too hard on her. All of us have kinfolk at home depending on us."

"Yes," Judith agreed thinly, "and yet none of us save her went over to the enemy. But someone tell me what happened."

Lydia sniffed and Lucy patted what seemed to be the bundle's shoulder. "Near as we can figure—it's come out only between sobs, you see—Abigail decided to ask if the mills would take her back, with that five-cent raise Mr. Boott promised," said Lucy. "She'd no sooner set out for the Boott Palace, however, than she felt a tug on her hair. Well, she turns around and no one is there. So, on she goes. A few steps more, and she feels it again. She looks around, but she's quite alone in the lane. Of course, now she feels queer and haunted, but cowardice won't feed her family, so on she goes, determined to ignore the tugging.

"Firmer and more frequent it grows, from all quarters, and she's sure she's under attack by spirits or worse. She goes running into town, covering her head as best she can with her arms. She meets Laura and Betsy returning with the groceries for Mrs. H, and begs them to shield her. Well, of course, they don't know what's going on, but Laura lends her a shawl to throw over her head, and she makes her way back here like that. Little enough good it did her."

"What do you mean?" Judith asked, blinking fast, unsure whether she credited Lucy's account or not. It certainly appeared Lucy believed it.

"Oh, show her, you ninny!" said Lydia, seizing the pillow from over Abigail's head. The girl's scalp appeared briefly, pale and bald in the dim firelight, before she pulled herself below the bedclothes again like a tortoise taking shelter.

All of Abigail's brunette locks were gone.

Judith clapped her hands over her open mouth. Had the spell—her spell, Hannah's spell—truly worked so well? She wheeled around to look at the Seer, to find that Hannah had sunk to the foot of the empty bed nearest the door, holding herself tightly and staring sightlessly into the corners of the room.

"What do you want to do with her?"

Lucy's question brought Judith back to the huddled traitor. "Do with her?"

"Some of the Union"—Lucy measured her tone precisely as a new bolt of cloth—"have a mind to run her out of Lowell. Others understand her reasons—they might even do the same if pressed to it—and say she's been punished enough."

"At least," said Lydia, all righteous fury, "we should show her head to the other boardinghouses, to see what happens to oath-breakers."

Judith gasped, for she felt much the same as Lydia. In a fortnight, had the gap between the staunch radical and the belle of Lowell narrowed so much?

"No one outside of this house has seen her or knows what's happened," Lucy explained. "We agreed to let you decide."

Judith scowled. "We can't parade her around—much as I'd like to, Lydia," she added, when the other girl's rose-bud mouth opened to object. "Surely, the tale of invisible demons plucking a girl bald won't serve our reputation any. That really might get someone hanged." She sighed and sat on the bed opposite Abigail, and pulled the quilt off the accused.

The miserable creature lifted her face, bald and tearful as a newborn.

"Abigail, are you sorry?"

"Sorry! Lord." The girl let out a bitter laugh. "Yes, I'm most contrite and regretful. I am sorry I ever met you, Judith Whittier, or that ginger-haired *witch*!"

Judith twisted to look for Hannah and saw the words hit the Seer with a force that doubled her over. Without a thought, Judith twisted back and let her hand fly, straight across Abigail's cheeks.

The blow landed with a crackling *smack*! At the same moment, a desperate cough exploded from Hannah's lungs. Startled, Lucy, Lydia, and Patience drew together in a circle around Abigail, clutching at one another's hands, while Judith rushed to Hannah's side. The first cough became a fit, ragged breaths sawing through the Seer's throat as she gasped.

"Hannah, Hannah," Judith soothed, patting her back. She could feel the older girl's ribs, even through her calico dress.

Hannah recovered, finally finding breath to sit up straight. She stared across the room at Abigail, who quailed, turned her gaze away, and began to cry again. Lucy sat down on the bed and yielded her shoulder for the miserable prisoner to cry into.

Judith's hand, with its banded pinky finger, rested on the Seer's shoulder. "If you put it to me," she began, "I say it's up to Hannah. What do you think we should do with her? Is she part of the Union, or isn't she?"

Hannah reached up and covered Judith's hand with her own. Her eyes shut once more.

"Part of the Union," wheezed the Seer. "She was only trying to protect her family."

The other girls—even Lydia—gave a sigh of relief.

Hannah stood up and moved for the door. Judith made as if to follow, but the Seer shook her off. "Apologize to her," Hannah murmured, gently pushing Judith away. "You're hungry and tired, and you didn't mean it."

Then Hannah left, leaving Judith standing clumsily before the weeping girl she had struck.

After a moment, Abigail swallowed. "It's all right. I didn't mean it, either," she said. "If there's none swifter, I know the Union is the better way to earn for my parents. I don't regret knowing you. Or Hannah." She rubbed tears off her cheeks, then settled her fingers on her head, pitifully feeling for the hair she must know was no longer there. It was strange, how domed and egg-like her pate. With her brunette locks intact, many would have called Abigail as beautiful as Sarah Payne or Lydia.

"It isn't so bad." Lucy chucked her on the chin. "Phrenologists are sure to discount your next reading."

Abigail moaned, while Patience and Lydia shook their heads at Lucy.

"I'll loan you a cap," said Judith, unable to force her mouth into words of any more contrite disposition.

8

Kitchen Magic

BREAD DOUGH SMACKED AGAINST the kitchen table with a great *thwap*, sending forth an explosion of floury smoke within which Mrs. Hanson might well have concealed herself, except that continuous muttering betrayed her position. In fresh curses she protested the crick in her neck, the fatigue in her feet, the indifference of young people, and the arrogance of rich. Most specially that great potentate of Lowell himself, Kirk Boott! Her fingers, so arthritic and unwilling as they kneaded the dough, itched to seize and twist the man's silk cravat until he choked. She might have known he'd turn their interview into an interrogation. More fool her, for marching upon him without reinforcements or artillery. A mistake she would not repeat.

At least no harm had yet come of it. For here was Hannah, gobbling her supper as hastily as any night, her narrow backside propped against the windowsill.

There'd been some fuss among the girls over that little

mouse Abigail North, who'd come in with Betsy and Laura and the groceries, a shawl over her head, and scurried upstairs at once. She did not reappear for supper. Mrs. Hanson felt no inclination to investigate; she had kept the Lowell house long enough not to involve herself in all the little dramas of her wards. One more plate of beans and gravy remained on the sideboard, for Abigail or Judith Whittier, whichever had the stomach to come for it. Hannah—Hannah the Gifted, Hannah the Fire-Kissed—never went to bed hungry. Well, house matrons (like mothers) were entitled to their favorites.

Four years earlier, when the ginger-haired maid came to Lowell, Mrs. Hanson had never seen a child so haunted. Hannah was mute among the robust crowd of girls at meal times, and first to retreat to the dormitories while the others took turns at checkers and cards. Finally, the matron told her that the washing-up after supper fell to the newest tenant in the house, and so drove her into the refuge of a task each evening. There, among the scrub brushes and buckets, Mrs. Hanson talked to her. Idle stories. Gossip from the Acre and English Row. The rising price of butter and the waste of modern fashions. The uselessness of Baptist and Methodist ministers alike. It was no more than the matron would have said to herself, if she were alone. She might as well have been, the ginger girl worked so silently.

Not until she witnessed Mrs. Hanson's tonics and po-
tions did Hannah speak up. One of the Sarahs was carried home from the mills fainting, and her friends begged
the matron not to call the doctor, who would charge
much, help little, and report every cough and shiver to
the corporation. Mrs. Hanson was not inclined to fetch
the man anyhow, but instead brewed a tea for
Sarah—Hemingway, she thought it was—to answer the
trouble. That night, the good woman discovered Hannah
staring into her cabinet of herbs as if to memorize every
leaf and root, except that her eyes were shut.

"You too can See the genius in things?" she asked,
when Mrs. Hanson nudged her to get on with the
washing.

"No," replied the matron. "I learned by rote. My great-
granddam could, or so the family lore tells me. But that
was a hundred years ago, on a different shore. Now you
tell me: what are you doing in a factory if you have the
gift?"

"Gift?"

"Your Sight."

"It is not a gift to me," the girl sighed. "My father was
a waterman on the Chesapeake where the tobacco farmers ship out; in my eighth year, I first witnessed a slave
auction there. One young man was standing on the block
when I shut my eyes—his soul shone orange like

embers—and the planters made their bids, one after another, until they'd conjured a thing that swallowed those burning embers in its mouth. . . . I howled so loudly, our congregation told my parents they must cast me out or be cast out themselves."

"What happened?"

"The family went west to start a new farm. In the winter, we slept all together in the one room, nine of us and the hogs and the cow, so not to freeze. I couldn't close my eyes, because I would See the succubae coiling around the necks of the animals." The girl shuddered.

"You cannot be near subjugated creatures, man nor beast," said Mrs. Hanson, recalling more of the ancient lore.

Hannah nodded. "My brothers and sisters froze anyway. All but my oldest brother, who escaped to sea. He sailed for two seasons on a whaling ship before he drowned."

"That's hard." Even now, the matron feared a similar end waiting for her first and fourth sons. "But how did you come to Lowell?"

"On the day my parents received the news, I started north. I knew they couldn't bear the sight of me any longer." As if her own sad history could no longer interest her, the girl reached out and fingered a jar of hazel bark. "You work magic blind?"

"I grope my way in the dark." The matron shrugged. "You See but you don't work it?"

"No one ever taught me. And I was afraid."

"Well. I can answer the first score and teach you what I know. On the second, I cannot help. I cannot make you brave." Mrs. Hanson put an arm around the ginger girl's thin shoulders, to soften the words. For truly, this was a wonder and a precious thing: to have a living Seer in her house. Mrs. Hanson blinked back tears even at the memory of the revelation.

Now the girl sat on the windowsill, masticating her plate of beans and coughing into the underside of her elbow when the phlegm and cotton dust proved too great a barrier to her lungs. She looked listless. Unsettled. Recalling Kirk Boott's questions, Mrs. Hanson wished she had a lesson to read the girl, a scheme of protection or undetectable attack, but they had sounded the depths of the matron's wisdom and found bottom some time ago.

And now here was Judith Whittier on the threshold, sniffing the air like a hound for whatever food might be on hand. *This one.* Mrs. Hanson smiled—could not forbear smiling—as she put the plate in the little bulldog's hand. At least Judith's name had not crossed Kirk Boott's lips that afternoon.

She dug in where she stood, too ravenous to complain that the beans were cold. Her fist around the spoon was stout and pugnacious as the rest of her, and Mrs. Hanson wondered what they had got up to today. Out in the parlor, sounds of the usual nightly diversions had crept back into the house, and someone was picking out notes on the piano, shaping a recognizable tune.

Mrs. Hanson returned to her kneading, singing to herself.

> *"There came a young man from the old countree,*
> *The Merrimack River he happened to see,*
> *What a capital place for mills, quoth he,*
> *Ri-toot, ri-noot, ri-toot, ri-noot, ri-umpty, ri-tooten-a."*

It was an old tune, but these lyrics told a tale not so ancient, well known to the farmers and goodwives in the hills around Lowell.

Meanwhile, the girls spoke to one another at last.

"Did I injure you?" Judith began.

"No." Hannah shook her head at once. "No. I only—I only wonder why you treated Abigail that way? You were so cold with her."

"She endangered the entire Union—she could have broken the strike—"

Now Mrs. Hanson gave up the final *ri-toot*. What was this?

"She couldn't," said Hannah, setting her empty plate

against the table with a clatter. "None of us could. It doesn't matter how many boardinghouses evict us, or whether our families starve, or we spend our last penny. *We can't end the strike, Judith.* That's how the spell works!"

Judith's features, close-packed in the center of her face and best suited to expressions of determination and doggedness, nevertheless gave their best impression of astonishment. "Of course. That was the objective—we cannot end it until the owners give in."

"And if they never do?"

"Then, when we decide—*all together*—we end it."

Hannah shook her head. "You don't realize, do you?"

"Realize what?"

"You spoke the spell." Hannah smudged a tear off her cheek. "I didn't know it would happen this way, but it gives you command of us. I could see it plain as day tonight."

"I didn't ask to be in command! I thought we were all equals in this endeavor."

Hannah smiled, a little chuckle escaping her lips.

"What is it?"

"It isn't a lie if you believe it's the truth."

Judith danced foot to foot.

"You have a very hard soul," said Hannah.

"*What?*"

"I only mean—I only mean that you could go on and on, much farther than the rest of us could. Or would." A coughing fit came over Hannah then, and she turned her head. Mrs. Hanson wanted to go to her, to thump her back and stroke her hair out of her face. Instead, she filled a cup of water and pressed it into the Seer's hands.

Meanwhile the other girl watched, wringing her hands. "So, the other girls want to end it," she said, "but they can't, because I don't. Is that it?"

"No." Hannah breathed in cautiously, testing her lungs. When no cough exploded back at her, she continued. "They don't want to end it, not yet. But I'm frightened for you. If we don't find a way to win soon, you'll be beset by enemies abroad and at home. Mr. Boott can't fail to notice you, and the other girls must begin to tire and fear. Abigail isn't the only operative with troubles."

Hannah wouldn't lie to spare Judith's feelings; she couldn't.

"Do you think I ought to end it?"

Upon discovering the question was meant for her, Mrs. Hanson's eyebrows rose. "And when has my opinion mattered?"

"You've been in Lowell longer than any of us," said Judith. "You've worked for *them* longest. You must know the enemy best. Can we outlast them?"

Always the little general. Mrs. Hanson sighed. "They

are looking for new girls to hire, and not only in Boston. And their pockets are far deeper than yours. Can the lot of you afford to stay out a week? A fortnight? A month? I cannot promise to feed you beyond that."

Judith's jaw hardened.

Hannah, the reedy young thing, threaded her arm through the matron's and put her head upon the older woman's shoulder. Tired and aching as her limbs might be, Mrs. Hanson suddenly felt quite stout, and patted the girl's pale hand.

"What is that song you were singing, Mrs. H?" Hannah asked.

"That's the ballad of your friend Mr. Boott. When the Boston gentlemen wanted to build their mills, 'twas he who spotted for them and noticed the might of the Merrimack below the falls. The only trouble was, the village of Chelmsford was already here, enjoying the rush of the river in pastoral simplicity. So, up he comes to the villagers, playing no more than a sheep rancher—and buys up their land for a trifle:

> *"And then these farmers so cute,*
> *They gave all their lands and timber to Boott.*

"Only after the mills were built, the people of Chelmsford knew what they'd given up."

"A dissembler through and through," said Judith, through her teeth.

"A clever businessman, he might say," said the matron.

"But it's all built on fictions and theft, isn't it? Boott stole the land. Old Mr. Lowell stole the looms—"

What other thefts the little radical might wish to enumerate would remain a mystery, however, for Hannah interjected a question. "What do you mean, 'stole the looms'? They're built here."

Unperturbed, Judith replied, "I mean the plans. Did you think our Boston overlords are clever enough to devise a machine of their own? No. Old Lowell crossed the sea just to spy on the Lords of Lancashire and copy their inventions, such as they are. The owners christened the new city 'Lowell' to honor his subterfuge. That's how the power loom reached these free shores."

If the Seer wished to know any more of this history, her inquiry was cut short, for another coughing fit overcame her. She released Mrs. Hanson in order to bend forward, her palms resting on her knees. While the matron winced at one girl's hacking, she nevertheless caught a glimpse of the other's face observing her friend keenly. How strange! Always in the past the parts were swapped: Hannah studying Judith as if she were a lesson Hannah meant to learn.

With a hand, the ginger girl gestured her desire for

a handkerchief, and Mrs. Hanson obliged before Judith could supply hers.

"I should fetch Dr. Green," said Judith, though the coughing abated.

"There's nothing to pay him," said Hannah.

"You ought to rest now," the matron advised. Mercifully, the Seer nodded, though her gaze lingered on Judith before passing and retreating out of the kitchen and up the stairs. The other girl moved to follow her co-conspirator, but the matron caught her with a stern glance.

"Wash up those plates, will you? I've already started on tomorrow's breakfast."

Reluctantly, the bulldog moved, retrieving the plates and spoons which she and Hannah had eaten off.

"Do you know," said the matron, as she dusted her fingers to take up rolling and smashing dough once more, "why I stuck you up in that room beside her when you arrived in Lowell, not a friend in the world?"

"To irritate Lydia at every opportunity?"

Mrs. Hanson smiled in spite of herself. "*She* asked for you. I'd just sent you down to the corporation to log your name with the paymaster, when she comes and tells me, 'Mrs. H, hers is the brightest soul I've ever Seen. If she is beside me, when I shut my eyes, it shall be like staring into the sun that blots out every other flame. All else will be darkness and calm.' Did you know? Did she never tell you how she manages to sleep when phantoms and demons live on the insides of her eyelids?"

The young bulldog had gone still. "I didn't know," she murmured.

"Think on that when you decide to keep the strike or not."

9

The Engineer's Tidings

HANNAH MAY HAVE FOUND a way to rest easy, but Judith slept fitfully that night. In her dreams, rows of idle machines and empty bobbins mingled with Abigail's bald head and Mrs. Hanson's skeptical eyebrows, Hannah's voice and Hannah's cough. Something had become uncorked inside Judith that day, a wellspring of soft feeling gurgling—gushing—in a dull ache. What could it mean? Judith didn't know what to do with her hands or legs.

Mindful of waking Hannah, she tried to keep still. The room was unbearably close and warm, with six hearts pushing hot blood through young limbs, and six sets of lungs exhaling into the shared atmosphere. At last, slick as a spent stage horse, Judith threw off the coverlet and let the night chill her into dead slumber.

A man came before dawn. Florry woke the house, shouting Judith's name until she came to the door of the dormitory and looked down. Through sleep-blurred eyes, Judith recognized the ruddy face and wide frame of

Mr. Reed, the engineer of the Merrimack Mills.

"New operatives are arriving today," he said as he stood at the bottom of the staircase, his face red in the light of the lantern he carried. "It's a flatboat from Boston, coming down the canal with a hundred Irish or more. Mr. Curtis said I'm to check the machines, get them running again."

At once Judith returned to her trunk, seeking the cleaner of her two dresses.

"Mr. Curtis gave me the order," said the engineer, alternately speaking to Florry, Lydia, and the other girls who had gathered on the staircase, "and I've no doubt he had it from Mr. Boott. You know I'm a working man myself; I don't hold your sex against you Union girls. But I can't disobey."

"Thank you, Mr. Reed, truly, for the warning," Judith called. "Hannah, wake up! The time is come!"

There was no response. Judith jumped back, startled to find the other side of their bed empty. "Where is she?"

"She was coughing a fit last night," said Lucy.

"I didn't hear it," Judith marveled. Or she'd thought it was only her dreaming.

"Mrs. Hanson did," said Florry, stirring the fire's embers to brighten the room. "They left the house about an hour ago. I saw them through the window. I thought only for fresh air, but they must have gone to the doctor."

The tightness in Judith's chest eased, but only a tick. If Mrs. Hanson had taken Hannah to Dr. Green, she must be very ill indeed.

Shucking off that worry, she glanced around, at Florry, Sarah Payne, and Lucy. Others were just beyond the room's door on the landing. Lydia, watching and waiting. Abigail, in her borrowed cap and tear-swollen eyes.

The looms, she wanted to say. *The looms are ours. They strike with us.* But that was a conundrum only half-solved, and without Hannah . . .

The bells of Lowell were ringing: half past four.

"What do we do, Judith?" asked Lucy.

"We must do something," said Abigail.

"We will," Judith replied at once. Half a solution was better than none at all. "First, we wake every Merrimack girl we can find, tell them come to the canal." She finished lacing her boots and tied her Union band firmly to her arm. *"We can still win this."*

10

Passions

"**THIS IS THE FILTHIEST** scene ever witnessed," Lydia told Judith. "Truly, only you could devise such a thing." All around them, operatives from the Merrimack Mill were strung along the edge of the headrace, expectorating like sailors. Their spittle flew through the air with lusty *Ptah!*s that made a counterpoint to the creaking and grinding of the mill wheel. As often as not, the projectiles landed on the cotton lying on the flat skiffs in the canal, but the true target, as Judith had explained, was the water flowing through the wheel, the lifeblood of the mill. The girls made a game of it, forgetting that overseers and matrons had ever admonished them to maintain virtuous deportment.

"It's all Hannah's craft. You"—Judith paused to add her own spittle to the unnatural rain—"gave her the idea."

"Me?" Lydia asked, after hurling her own with all the force her rosebud lips could muster.

"What you said kissing the shuttle," Judith replied, "when we wove that first night."

"Oh," Lydia replied, surprised, as if she hardly expected Judith to remember a word she said. "Something about kissing no other men?"

"Yes," Judith nodded. "Hair is the perfect vessel for oaths of friendship and camaraderie. Blood for family. But spit"—she added another drop of her own—"is for the passions. We've been kissing our machines for so long—"

"And you expect the machines to behave like faithful paramours?"

Judith nodded. Lydia shook her head, but she could not forbear a smile. If any girl knew the power of holding a lover enthralled, it must be Lydia.

"Hannah and I have circled every mill in Lowell, saying the incantations, bidding the looms to weave for no others."

"And this?" Lydia asked, gesturing to the expectorating mob around them.

"To invoke the spell." Judith smiled, leaving out that Hannah had left her with no confidence of its efficacy, while the looms still belonged to the Boston owners.

"Look there!" shouted someone on Judith's left.

The sun's first light was paling from orange to yellow, casting its rays over a phalanx of men in working cottons, marching over the footbridge. Judith shielded her eyes to see them properly. It was twenty or more of the mill hands, to move the cotton bales from the warehouses to the carding and spinning rooms, and finally from the backlogged skiffs. Judith thought of Mr. Reed, unhappily following orders. Even now, the girls might delay the men and convince them to join their striking sisters.

She lost that hope when she spotted what looked like an English dandy among them. Mr. Boott marched at the head of the crowd in a dark jacket and pale pants—stirrupped below his shoes so as not to break the pleasing line of the leg. A magpie among wrens.

"Stop! You there! Girl! Stop that!" he shouted. Many of the girls ignored him, or were so carried away in the pleasure of spitting on the corporation's property, they had yet to notice they were caught. Around him, the working men were a buzz of confusion and uncertainty.

The overseer, Mr. Curtis, added his own exulting shout, "Little hussies, there's no escape for you now!"

Judith's blood rose, though she realized at once that Mr. Curtis might, in the strictest sense, be correct. With the mill walls behind them and the men blocking the bridge, there was no escape aside from trying their luck in the canal's current.

"I can't swim," Lydia informed her.

"No need," said Judith. "We've done what we came here to do." She edged past Lydia, careful not to lose her footing on the pitched stones of the headrace, and made for the footbridge. "Come along. Come along," she murmured to the others.

Mr. Curtis stepped into her path. On her first day in Lowell, it was he who'd stood over her while she signed away her waking hours to the Merrimack Corporation, while Hannah was petitioning Mrs. Hanson to board them together.

"Judith Whittier. I might have guessed. Where's your ginger shadow?"

She blinked, breathed, and looked up into Curtis's familiar, rheumy blue eyes and that long, crooked nose, which he enjoyed sticking into the girls' faces if ever he caught them daydreaming. The weavers fancied he'd tried it once with a male hand, who punched him hard and fast, giving the nose its permanent crook.

Judith wished she had the strength and reach to do the same. Her face was barely higher than Curtis's chest, which was not over-broad but thick and immovable enough.

"My friends are going to pass," said Judith.

For a long moment, no one stirred. Mr. Curtis smirked.

"*My friends,*" Judith repeated, louder, hoping at least one of her fellows would take her meaning, "*are going to pass.*"

Behind her, at last, she felt another girl—it might have been Abigail North—test her words and press by. Curtis didn't move, but the working men opened room for her along the bridge.

"What? No!" Beside the overseer, Mr. Boott sputtered like a water pump. "Stop them!"

Other girls followed Abigail, flowing through the group of men like fog through silent trees. Judith felt the girls go one by one as she held Mr. Curtis's gaze. It was as if she were one knot in a loosely woven net: she felt a tug on her scalp as each girl passed, and yet she was unmoved.

"Stop them! Arrest them!" Mr. Boott continued to shout, until one of the men finally spoke up.

"Sir, we're outnumbered five to one."

Feeling the last of her comrades pass through the ranks of the working men, Judith let a smile turn her lips. "Good day, Mr. Curtis," she said. "Mr. Boott." She nodded to the agent and prepared to depart.

It was Boott who stepped into her path this time, desperate to compose himself as he straightened the cravat that bloomed below his chin. Judith held in a laugh. Did he think he could frighten her where Curtis could not?

"It doesn't matter," he said aloud, though whether to Judith or Curtis or the general crowd, he himself perhaps didn't even know. "All of you witches will be arrested soon enough."

"Witches?" Judith replied. "We mill girls are God-fearing churchgoers. As much is written into our contracts." Which was quite right: to keep her place, every girl in Lowell was required to attend one church or other on Sunday.

Truthful as her words might be, without the other girls at her back, Mr. Boott and the men around him had no trouble keeping Judith on the bridge. "I know all about your wicked spells now." His hand seized the band around her arm. "And they won't work any longer, not without the queen of your coven. That one is already in custody."

He gave a yank, to tear the band off her arm. The force wrenched her shoulder, and she felt herself stumbling precariously on the edge of the bridge. To avoid falling, she seized Mr. Boott's shoulders. Still the woven band would not yield.

When she'd righted herself, she stepped backward, until she had both the agent and the overseer in view, Boott sweating below his wig and Curtis smirking at her—

They had someone in custody.

Hannah!

Judith lowered her head and charged between the two men at the front of the crowd. Boott and Curtis shouted again, but she had already pressed into the knot of working men and was dodging her way across the bridge. The mill hands were far less interested in keeping her there than the gentry of Lowell, and cleared a way as quickly as they could.

Hannah Hannah Hannah, beat Judith's heart. She met the lane, turned on her heel, and ran. That weasel Curtis must have told Boott to suspect Hannah, if Judith were leading the strike. How many times must he have seen them together, walking arm in arm through the gates, or stealing a moment of fresh air on the staircase between weaving rooms? But Mr. Boott had called Hannah a witch, and he *couldn't* have heard so much from Curtis, who didn't know about Hannah's Sight and certainly couldn't know about their spell-making. Unless one of the other mill girls—

A knot of the other Unionists were waiting for her not far, ready to embrace her for her courage. "You were wonderful!" Georgie beamed.

"What's the matter?" asked Lydia.

"Hannah!" Judith gasped, without pausing. Could one of them have betrayed her? No—the spell must prevent that treason as it prevented Abigail from returning to the mills.

Judith shook her head. Finding Hannah was the task at hand. Where would they keep her? Lowell had no jail. Perhaps the post office?

Mary Paul, the Vermonter from the Lawrence Mills, caught her by the hand, running in the opposite direction. "The new workers!" She gasped. "New workers coming down the river!"

Distinctly, Judith could feel the threads of the Union pact tugging at her, pulling her toward the dock.

"Tell the other girls to spit," she told Mary, resisting. "Spit in the river. Spit in the canal."

"Spit?"

"Ask Lydia!" Judith called over her shoulder. Like a shuttle passing through warp threads, she went dodging lines of her fellow mill girls, who were gathering under the poplars that followed the canal. *They* are *the warp,* she thought. *And Hannah and I—we are the weft.*

She let her feet take her, following, she realized at last, the path to the Boott Palace itself.

~

Perspiring and bewildered, Judith stepped into the shade of the columned porch and stopped. Nervously, her hands rose, and she turned the braided ring of Hannah's and her own hair around her pinky finger.

Surely, whomever Mr. Boott had left on guard would not simply hand over the prisoner. Perhaps Judith ought to fetch Mrs. Hanson from the boardinghouse, to plead their cause. Perhaps she ought to have gathered some of the operatives to assist her.

Before she could think any further, the door swung open, revealing the figure of Dr. Green and his medical bag.

A voice spoke from the interior of the house. "Thank you, Doctor, yes, we'll be sure she gets fresh air."

"See that she does," the doctor replied, exiting reluctantly. As the door began to swing shut behind him, Judith darted forward and stuck her foot between the door and the lintel.

"Doctor," she said brightly. "Thank you so much for coming."

Her appearance startled both the doctor and Mrs. Hanson, who proved to be the owner of the voice from within. Judith paused to stare.

None of the mill girls had betrayed them. Mrs. Hanson knew as much as they did about the spellcraft, but the boardinghouse keeper was under no bond of loyalty to the Union.

Recovering her presence of mind, Judith spoke to the doctor. "Poor Hannah kept us up all night with her coughing. But Mr. Boott has been so kind to look after her personally, and Mrs. Hanson is one of the Lord's own angels."

Dr. Green looked between the mill girl and the matron, as if he trusted neither, but both smiled back benignly, and Judith slid over the threshold with the grace of a cat slipping into forbidden rooms. Mrs. Hanson couldn't very well stop her while the doctor was watching.

"I'll leave you to it, then," said Dr. Green. "Good day, young lady. Mrs. Hanson."

After thanking the man, Judith took the door and shut it, sealing herself inside the Boott Palace. At once she turned on the matron.

"You traitorous hag!"

The older woman backed away, raising her hands before her face in the nick of time, before Judith's claws could reach her cheeks.

"All that talk about Hannah's gift! All your awe for magic, and old ways, and your granddam the wise woman! All while spying and sneaking and preparing to betray us!"

Judith landed a flurry of blows on the matron's arms before, with a quickness and strength that belied her age, Mrs. Hanson caught the girl's wrists and held her firm.

"What did you think, my girl?" Mrs. Hanson's face was harder than Judith had ever seen it, and she shook the younger woman to rattle her teeth in her head. "That one coin from Georgie's family could keep thirty mouths fed? That I run a charity house, with no belly nor family of my own to think of? I have daughters, married off younger than you are now; they risk their lives in childbed every year, to please their husbands. I have sons, who'll die at sea like as not. Call Sunday the Lord's day if you want to, I never had a day of rest in my life, not from work and not from trouble. You radicals—I ought to sell the lot of you and hire myself out to witch for the corporations when the next cotton mouse gets it in her head to strike. Least then, I might hold two dimes to rub together before I'm dead."

Judith was stupefied. In all her grumbling, all her muttering, Mrs. Hanson had never said so much to one of her boarders, and all Judith could do was burst into tears.

Mrs. Hanson was shocked enough to let her go. "What are you crying for?"

"Where's Hannah? I need Hannah."

The matron groaned and shook her head. "In there." She pointed, then, seeing that the younger woman's tears hadn't stopped, took Judith's hand and led her through a parlor that was as unlike the matron's own as an oyster to a pearl. The walls were papered in pale green, to match the sofas and the gold-and-green carpets, and the golden frames around the portraits of Mr. Boott and his wife.

Beyond this room opened a library, with a writing desk and a row of pigeonholes and looming bookcases, which must serve as the agent's workplace when he was at home. Inside, a figure clad in a white shift and surrounded by long locks of coppery hair was unrolling papers one-handed.

"Hannah?" Judith brushed tears off her cheeks.

The Seer turned, dropped a handkerchief pressed to her mouth to smile at Judith, and immediately lifted it again. She made the cruelest hacking sound ever heard. Judith ran to her.

"Judith," she wheezed, "good. Help me. We must find the plans." Her voice had hardly enough vigor in it to make out words; Judith couldn't think what she was talking about.

"Hannah, I must get you away from here, and then you must rest. You're ill, you're—" When Hannah dropped the handkerchief again, Judith saw a vivid spot of blood, red against the white cotton.

"There isn't time," Hannah wheezed. "Mr. Boott will return soon to question me. He wants me to denounce all the Union as witches. Of course, our spell won't let me, but he hardly knows that." Her coughing turned into laughter and back into coughing. "Help me." She pulled yet another roll of paper from the desk and thumbed through the pages.

"What are you looking for?" Judith asked at last. "Plans?" Meanwhile, Mrs. Hanson had picked up a piece of chalk and was drawing a ring on the floor to encircle both girls and the desk. "What is happening?"

Hannah had to hack and spit in Mr. Boott's inkwell before she answered. "Our spell. There!" She unrolled a sheaf and weighted the papers on the desk with a brass candlestick.

Hannah shut her eyes, in the gesture Judith knew meant she was using her Sight to examine the document; unable to do the same, Judith squinted with her very ordinary gaze. The script was too fine to read at a glance, but the illustrations were clear.

"Looms?" she asked.

Hannah's hair had never spread more wildly about her as she opened her eyes and met Judith's gaze. "It's as you said. Many years ago, the city's namesake, Mr. Lowell, went spying all the way to England and took down the plans, then claimed the patents here." She stretched out her free hand to Judith, and Judith took it. "This is the papercraft that gave the corporations mastery over our looms. I can See it now: this is how they conjured it."

Judith's heart beat faster, as she began to understand Hannah's meaning. "Conjured what?"

"The great maw that lurks in each machine, swallowing up our labor and our lives, that returns nothing."

The vision chilled Judith in spite of herself, but the pressure of Hannah's fingers on her own, and the new horizon of understanding, filled her with a trembling joy. "Can we make the spell work? Can we make the looms faithful to us?"

"They were seduced away from their owners once. Why not again?" Hannah could say no more, as coughing overcame her again.

Mrs. Hanson came around again, this time placing candles along the ring she had traced, five in all. Judith caught the matron's eye. "You aren't a traitor, are you?"

"Oh, I am," the older woman grunted, straightening up. "But it's not you I betrayed. Only Boott and my own good sense."

"Why did you say all that, then?"

"What would you say to an enraged harpy scratching at your eyes?"

Judith swallowed, as the unpleasant sensation of an apology owed overtook her. "I . . . Please, I didn't . . ."

"Don't go on and on. Goodness! You're more fool-hardy than I thought if you never suspected I'd give you up. I thought about it more than once. Then this one up and *asks* me to."

Judith looked at Hannah sharply. Hannah gave another small cough and lifted one shoulder. "I couldn't think of another way into Mr. Boott's sanctum. I was coughing a fit last night, but I convinced Mrs. Hanson to take me here instead of the doctor's."

"But I saw Dr. Green. You aren't pretending, Hannah, that's real blood—"

The Seer nodded. "I'm dying," she said, between coughs, "so I need you to kiss me quickly."

The two phrases met Judith's ears like fists, making her vision swim, and she reached out to hold Hannah by the shoulders, both to keep her feet and to be sure that the other girl was real. "That's neither a thing to joke about."

Hannah dropped the handkerchief on the desk so that she could take a lit taper from Mrs. Hanson. "When have you ever known me to joke?" To the five candles now blazing along the ring, she added the sixth, in the brass candlestick atop the plans of the power looms. She leaned in close to Judith. "These machines need an example." Her clean hand touched Judith's chin, tilting her face up slightly. "May I?"

With new tears in her eyes, Judith nodded.

11

God in His Heaven

SPITTING!

Still!

The display that morning at the bridge was but an overture. From his vantage at a sixth-floor window of the Merrimack Mill, Mr. Boott could see dozens more operatives ranged along the banks of the canal, expectorating into the current.

He couldn't stop them. There weren't loyal men enough in Lowell both to prevent the young women from making beasts of themselves *and* to escort the new operatives to the mills as they arrived from Boston. If not for the escorts, these striking hellcats might well attack the fresh workers. Or corrupt them.

"It's only spittle," said Curtis, as the overseer approached from behind. Under his command, dozens of men were downstairs, unloading, cleaning, and carding the bales of cotton, engaged in productive work after weeks of idleness. Clerks were already interviewing the first of the new girls, giving them contracts and assigning them a place in the spinning and weaving rooms.

Mr. Boott turned, overlooking the overseer to gaze instead at row upon row of power looms, like soldiers at attention. Even amidst the present trial, he allowed himself a moment's reflection on the majesty of the integrated factory: every step from cotton boll to cut-and-dyed fabric, under one roof and one corporation, bottom to top. Truly, Man, whose mind could design such marvels, was made in the image of God.

The reflection made Curtis's dismissive words all the more irritating. "It's witchcraft," said Mr. Boott. "It's unnatural."

"Then hang these mules," said Curtis. "The new girls will start and no one will mind. Or at least hang Judith Whittier and her ginger friend, and let the rest beg for their jobs again."

"Judith who?" asked Mr. Boott, ignoring, for the moment, that he had no license to hang anyone. That would have to wait for the magistrate from Boston.

"The ringleader. The one who challenged me on the bridge."

The same girl (Mr. Boott thought) who had handed him the operatives' demands at his doorstep. He would have to question the matron Hanson and the self-proclaimed Seer about her.

Newcomers were climbing into the weaving from the staircase—one of Curtis's hands, and then a pack of young women, ill-fed Irish by the look of them. Mr. Boott watched from his post at the window while Curtis joined his man to assign them to their looms, just one machine to a girl to start out. That was more lost time and profits; experienced weavers could manage three or four machines at a time.

Mr. Boott watched Curtis explain the harnesses and take-on rolls. The new girls assented in brogue voices that put Mr. Boott in mind of foggy days and endless moors. He had never been in Ireland itself but observed plenty of its people when he visited Lancashire. Well, these "lassies" would be glad of the regular wages and clean accommodations this side of the ocean.

At last Curtis returned to the front of the room, lifting a crook to reach the catch and affix the room's machines to the power belt and thereby to the might of the water-wheel below.

Now! thought Mr. Boott, with bated breath. Looms would channel river power; girls would tend the looms. God was in His Heaven, and all was right with the world.

Ka-thunk ka-thunk ka-thunk. The machines commenced their industrious song, the heddles danced while the shuttles darted between. The overseer and his assistant roved up and down the rows, minding the new girls minding the looms. Squinting, Mr. Boott could see the beginnings of a hundred new yards of cotton cloth, and sighed.

Twang! Thwap! No sooner had Mr. Boott released that puff of breath than there came from every quarter ghastly sounds. Several weavers screamed. Others ducked to the floor, as if they faced a division of firing Redcoats.

Mr. Boott stood dumbstruck.

"What's this?!" Curtis demanded from the far corner of the weaving room, but his words thundered across every row. "What's this!?" He advanced to the nearest loom. Half a dozen warp threads snapped like over-wound harp strings. At once he grabbed two of the offending ends, attempting to tie them together again. But finding the work too fine for his fingers, he seized the stunned maid who was meant to be minding the contraption and thrust her hands to the task instead.

"Tie! Tie!" he ordered.

The next girl shouted something incomprehensible, and the first yelped and pulled her hands back, sparing herself a nasty bruise at least as the shuttle came darting across. Curtis did *not* escape injury, as the power belt on the loom beside him snapped, lashing him across the temple.

Curtis's man, meanwhile, moved desperately up and down the rows, throwing the brake at one machine after another as more threads broke, belts slipped, and heddles jammed against one another, creating an uncomfortable, smoky friction as they continued striving. The braver and more industrious girls learned by example and threw the braking levers themselves.

Curtis bellowed with rage, clutching at his wounded head. His man gave up on singling out the offending machines and ran for the front of the room. Lifting the overseer's crook once more, he decoupled the entire fleet from the river's might.

At last the room quieted. Mr. Boott clutched his heart.

Above him, the power belt continued to spin as if nothing extraordinary had happened. Below, bobbins lay over the floor. The girls who had attempted to follow Curtis's instructions to repair the broken threads were tangled up, witless kittens in yarn.

At the nearest machine, the snow-white warp hung loose from the harnesses like a cobweb in a doorframe. Beside it cowered a blond maiden, a stranger to Lowell, likely on her very first day of paid work.

She wept like she'd seen the Devil himself.

12

Hannah's Genius

JUDITH PRESSED HER PALMS to Hannah's cheeks as she pulled away, lacking breath more than enthusiasm for the cause. The wellspring inside her had become a geyser; she wanted to hug and kiss, to invade with a singularity of purpose she was accustomed to feeling only from righteous indignation.

For her part, the Seer's face was pale as Mrs. Hanson's good china, yet the kisses and the witchcraft they were weaving together seemed to have put color in her cheeks and her lips.

"Who are you in love with, Judith?"

"You witch," Judith gasped, tears springing again, "you know full well!"

Hannah smiled at Judith and bit her bottom lip in the most irresistible ways. And she collapsed.

Judith shouted and strove to catch her beloved, only managing to wrestle Hannah into a slump against her shoulder, while she pressed her hip into Mr. Boott's desk for leverage. "Hannah!" Judith patted her pale cheek, and the Seer's eyelids fluttered, but for the rest, she was insensible.

"Wait, hold her still," Mrs. Hanson ordered sharply, taking time to blow out the candles before letting Judith cross the chalk circle or entering herself. "Now, then." She stepped forward and took Hannah's face between her palms.

Judith panted anxiously. "Is she . . . ?" she asked, when she could not wait any longer.

"Don't be foolish," said Mrs. Hanson. "She's only exhausted. But if she keeps on like this, forcing out magic when her fires are burning so low—"

"Her looms!" Judith interjected.

"What about them?"

"Hannah said that working in the mills, she could See her genius going into her looms; she said it was like watching her own breath sucked away! What if I could get it out again?"

Mrs. Hanson frowned. "Even if you can get her there before one or both of you are arrested, what spell will you invoke? I cannot tell you. I'm no—"

"But will you help me get her there?" Fortunately, Judith had never made any promise of honesty to Mrs. Hanson, because she certainly would not have liked to admit that she had no special plan or knowledge either.

The matron looked between the two of them, Hannah

quite unhearing and Judith quite desperately listening, before she nodded. "Very well. But we'd best clear this mess first, or Mr. Boott really will see you both hanged. Bring the chalk and the candles."

~

They moved slowly, for they had to hold Hannah up between them, one of her arms draped across Judith, the other over Mrs. Hanson's elderly shoulders. They had only reached the top of the lane when they spotted Mr. Boott himself, at the head of a crowd. There were Curtis and other overseers, as to be expected, but also Reverend Miles of St. Anne's and several of the boardinghouse keepers, and girls Judith was sure she had never seen before. Beside them were members of the Factory Girls' Union, easy to spot with their flowing hair and their armbands. Were *they* marching with Mr. Boott now too?

No. A few of the men had mill girls by the arm or the hair, forcing them along, and the other Union girls were trying to reach their captured comrades. At once, Judith felt a distinctive tug, urging her to run and help, but Hannah's weight held her to the spot.

Mr. Boott called out, "There they are, Reverend, the Devil's brides!"

The reverend, leaning heavily on his walking stick,

waved in their direction. "Is that Mrs. Hanson I see? Good lady, tell us the meaning of this?"

"They've bewitched the mills!" Mr. Boott interrupted. "The belts keep slipping, the rolls won't wind, the looms miss every other pick!" He marched directly to Judith, his cravat askew, his jabbing finger stopping just short of her chest. "You did this!"

Judith spoke into the cravat, because his face was an ugly thing without his customary decorum. "I won't be charged for a crime you cannot prove."

"Hah! *Cannot* . . . ? And what of your friends expectorating all morning, what of the machines' behavior, what of the threads snapping on the harnesses? Are we to believe these all coincidence? Reverend, you hear, you see—"

"Do you want to destroy Lowell, Mr. Boott?"

The question came from Lydia. With Abigail and Lucy alongside, she had fought her way to the front of the crowd, and now she addressed the agent herself, sleek black hair and rosebud lips as beguiling as ever.

"Careful, young lady. I'll see these two flogged before the day is out; I won't scruple to add a third."

"If you ever want so much as a bolt of cloth out of Lowell again, you'll sign and agree to our demands," said Lydia, producing a fresh copy out of her pocket.

"What demands?"

"You've seen them," said Abigail, who'd lost her cap

somewhere, leaving her bald head exposed. "We are the Factory Girls' Union of Lowell."

"There's hundreds of us," added Eliza, of the Concord Mills, "and not a one will work until you and your masters agree."

Mr. Boott wouldn't have it. "We have already hired new operatives—"

"Who can't use a single one of your machines. No one can, save us and those we choose to," said Lydia.

It worked, then. Judith couldn't have been sure until she heard it from one of her sisters' mouths. "The spell worked," she whispered to Hannah, who gave no sign she could hear.

"Nonsense," said Mr. Boott. "I'll hang these two if I have to and break their glamour."

"Go ahead!" said Lucy—a bit too enthusiastically for Judith's taste. "Flog them, hang them, drown them like rats. It won't change the facts: we are the ones who poured our sweat and souls into your looms. We have rights to expect a little loyalty."

"Reverend?" Mr. Boott tried desperately.

"Well, it isn't—it doesn't—it *could* be Satan's work, but—"

"Satan's work or not, you won't free yourselves from the laborers of Lowell unless you raze the town and start again somewhere else. We're in the mills and in the river, and we'll get ours back again if it's the last thing we do."

Judith had never expected such a speech to leave Lydia's mouth, of all people. Lucy clapped her on the back, but Abigail hadn't moved, staring at Mr. Boott.

The agent snapped like dry thread.

His face turned from purple as a beet to white as cotton. Judith knew he must be imagining what he would have to tell his employers now, that all their machines and their industrial town were useless without the striking girls. Well, wasn't that his job: conveying unpleasant messages to powerful men?

"Now," asked Lydia, wafting the paper before him, "are you ready to discuss our demands?"

Mr. Boott gave the merest of nods. Ever the gentleman, however, he offered Lydia his arm. "Shall we ... shall we discuss it over tea?"

Judith hadn't moved, nor had Hannah, nor Mrs. Hanson. As she passed with Mr. Boott, flanked by Abigail and Eliza now, Lydia caught Judith's eye with a questioning look, to which Judith nodded. "Well done," she mouthed.

The party had no sooner passed than the other girls of Mrs. Hanson's house and Mr. Reed the engineer ran to Judith.

"What's happened to her?" Lucy asked, while the kind man lifted Hannah.

"Please," said Judith, "I need to get her to her looms."

13

The Power Loom

MR. REED CARRIED THE SEER across the footbridge and through the gates of the Merrimack Mill. Judith walked quickly at his side, carrying the candles from Mr. Boott's house. Someone had begun ringing the bells in the Concord Mills, and soon the Lawrence Mills were answering, and even the bells of St. Anne's Church.

But the joyous clanging scarcely pierced Judith's ears. "Which looms are hers?" she asked Lucy, who worked in the same weaving room on the fifth floor. The machines stood, for now, in silent rows, abandoned by the replacement weavers.

Lucy led them past her own station, where she'd pasted up pages of Miss Wheatley's book to study while she worked, and showed them the four looms that Hannah had tended for untold hours.

"What about a doctor?" asked Florry, uneasy. "Surely, this is the worst place for her?"

"She needs her spirit back," said Judith. "She's spent

more of it here than any other place." She began making a circle, setting a candle down at each of the four looms and a final spot, where, "You can set her here, Mr. Reed," she said.

The square-shouldered engineer hesitated, eying the chalk circle she'd drawn. "Is it true? Is this all witchcraft?"

Before Judith could answer, Mrs. Hanson interceded. "It is craft, yes. To save someone we love very much. Isn't that the most Christian of acts?"

Finally, the man nodded and lay Hannah on the floor beside the fifth candle, crossing himself as soon as his hands were free.

Judith sighed and turned. "Sarah, would you?"

Sarah Payne nodded and began lighting the candles. Meanwhile, Judith stepped inside the circle, wondering what kind of incantation would spring to her lips. She'd never worked any craft without the Seer's directions.

Metaphor and connection, Hannah had said. *Spells were built on metaphor and connection.*

"Looms," Judith started, haltingly, "you know Hannah Pickering. With her hands, she's strung your heddles. With her eyes, she's minded your passes. With her fingers, she's tied your broken threads. With her lips, she's kissed your shuttle."

The others stood on the outside of the circle, watching and listening silently. Waiting. Quite unlike herself, Judith felt abashed in the center of their attention as she extemporized. Hannah let out a sharp cough that stood out from her wheezing, and Judith shook herself. She could not be cowed by uncertainty while Hannah needed her. Besides, the ears of the looms would not be critical.

"Toiling here, in this mill, in her every breath," she went on, "she gave up her youth to you. You drank in her soul, her genius."

Hannah coughed louder, heaving. She curled onto her side toward Judith and hacked into the crease of her elbow. Instinct told Judith to go to her, to comfort her beloved while her lungs struggled, but the spell was incomplete.

"She fed you cotton thread and her very breath. What did you give her in return?" Judith asked, growing louder. "You rendered up cloth but not to her—your finest gift you reserved for masters you've never known."

A startling sound—a groan—passed through the machines around them. Some of the girls reached for one another's hands.

"She *did* bewitch the machines," Florry whispered, as if she could never have believed it before.

"Shh," said Mrs. Hanson.

Judith licked her lips. Hannah was coughing harder than ever. "All you gave to Hannah was your dusty breath," Judith went on, raising her voice still higher.

It sounded as if all the looms were groaning now, in cascading echoes through the factory, though their gears remained still and the shuttles motionless.

Suddenly, Hannah pulled herself upright and sat at the fifth point of the circle. Air entered her lungs in long, ragged breaths between each cough.

"We need to get her out of here," murmured Sarah Payne. "She needs fresh air."

"You took her genius!" Judith accused, still louder, over Hannah's coughing. Indeed, it seemed that Hannah would surely do some injury to herself, forcing her lungs to toil so ferociously. And yet she was upright—she was awake—she was alive.

"Judith," Lucy tried, "I believe Sarah is right—"

"Wait," said Mrs. Hanson. "Judith, keep going."

"You took her genius!" Judith repeated, shouting now. The whole mill creaked and groaned like a storm-battered ship. Hannah's brow was wet with sweat and her hair was crimson. "*GIVE IT BACK!*"

Hannah collapsed, bracing herself against the floor, one hand on either side of the candle, while she gave a fierce, wet cough that sent a shudder through her entire form. Below her, a fist-sized boll of cotton hit the floor. An instant later, the five candles were snuffed out together. All became silent and still.

Judith's eyes went dark and she felt her knees buckle.

She sank to the center of her circle. After a moment, she felt cool, soft hands on her hot ones. A lock of copper hair dropped into view as her vision came back.

"Hannah?" she breathed, looking up into the heart-shaped face. "Are you all right?"

In response, the older girl took a long, deep breath and exhaled slowly. She smelled of the river after a rainfall and blooming columbine. She smelled clean.

The others broke the circle, rushing in to embrace their comrades, but it did not matter. There was no further need of craft today.

~

It was the first of May, and the townspeople of Lowell and not a few of the old Chelmsford farmers gathered on the lawn of the Boott Palace, watching the former agent's possessions make their way one by one from the house to the waiting wagon. It was the sole opportunity, for many, to marvel at the bronze candlesticks, the Japann'd tea service, the harpsichord, the heaps of silken garments trimmed in ermine and lace.

Among the onlookers stood a trio of gentlemen in high collars and starched cravats, mill owners come from Boston on the morning coach, to witness for themselves the departure of their former employee. Reportage of the mill girls' strike was confused and contradictory, but abundantly clear was Boott's innocence in the outcome. Nevertheless, neither Mr. Appleton of the Merrimack Corporation, nor the Lawrences of the eponymous mills, nor any of the absent owners could overlook a contract that bound them to a multiplying payroll, with absurd capital outlays in comfort and ventilation. An example must be made.

Around them, the people of Lowell carried on like revelers at a picnic, pointing and gossiping.

"Take heart, gentlemen," Mr. Appleton whispered to his companions, "this anarchy will not last. Already my southern friends apply themselves to our problem."

"*Our* problem," replied Amos Lawrence, grinding his teeth, "and it ought to be our solution."

"My brother means to say," said Abbott Lawrence, taking a milder tone, "is that we train a different species of labor altogether in Massachusetts. Unless you mean to import slavery?" he added, with a sniff of distaste.

"Never fear. You may continue to play the abolitionist," Mr. Appleton replied quietly, for Mr. Boott himself was emerging from the house, the blameless Mrs. Boott at his side, red-eyed below her bonnet. "Still, we might learn from the planters' example."

For the last time, the erstwhile agent turned the key in the lock and surrendered it to Mr. Appleton.

Alone among the onlookers, the trio of Boston gentlemen shook Boott's hand and wished him well. Near the coach, someone struck up a song, and not a few of the farmers and townsfolk joined in, a new verse to the old tune:

> *"Up came a thunder from each and ev'ry mill part,*
> *That clever old Boott shook and shuddered in heart,*
> *and he ran from the factory girls and their art!"*

Appleton turned to the Lawrences, proposing to resume their ad hoc conference. "Gentlemen," he spoke, as the chorus of *Ri-toot, ri-noot, ri-toot, ri-noot, ri-umpty, ri-tooten-a* chased away the Bootts' coach, "what do you know of conjuring?"

~

Meanwhile, into the late hours of the afternoon (but not, now, beyond six o'clock), the weavers tended their looms. On the sixth floor of the Merrimack Mill, Lydia managed five at once, matching Sarah Payne beside her; no easy feat, but between the two of them, they covered their own and the looms which belonged rightly to Judith.

"Damn!" Lydia shouted, throwing the brake on one

machine, loud enough that Patience, from two rows over, inquired, "What is it?"

"Nothing," Lydia clucked, examining the offending loom's shuttle. One of Judith's, of course—though the machines ran for Lydia, still they could be trying as their mistress. "Missed a pick. And I've run out of weft. Bobbin girl!"

At the summons, little Emelie Adams, now returned to Lowell with her sister after the strike's satisfactory conclusion, came running with fresh thread.

"Are you going back to Mrs. H for dinner, or to the Acre again?" Patience called over from her looms to Lydia.

"Back to the Acre. And who's coming with me? Someone's got to show these newcomers how to twist a spell, or they'll be no wiser than babes in arms when the next Boott arrives." As she spoke, Lydia exchanged the empty bobbin for the full, not forgetting to caress the shuttle fondly as she did.

"I'll go," said Sarah Payne.

"I'll go!" said little Emelie. "I want to learn! And meet the Irish."

"They're no stranger than Vermonters," Lydia warned the younger girl.

"What about our Seer?" asked Patience. "Oughtn't she explain witchcraft to them?"

Lydia shrugged a shoulder. "She'll come when she's able."

One floor below, Lucy and Abigail similarly took on looms in addition to their own, holding the place for their absent sister.

~

At the boardinghouse, in a show of favoritism that was sure to cause resentment sooner or later, Mrs. Hanson had abandoned her rear bedroom to Hannah while she convalesced. When the matron wasn't keeping Judith busy with sweeping and laundry, the little radical was there as well.

Though the strike was over, she still wore her armband, and the ring she and Hannah had braided together.

"The others are back at work, so should you be," Hannah said. Tucked in high and all alone in the four-poster, which had once been Mrs. Hanson's dowry, she appeared even more singular a creature than ever. Judith shivered to think that she'd had the self-assurance to touch her, much less kiss her on the lips.

"I want to know you rest peacefully."

"I do. I can," said Hannah, and she closed her eyes, to prove it. "There's nothing, only darkness." She breathed deeply, exhaled long and relaxed, and opened her eyes again. Bit by bit, her cheeks were gaining color. Her fever had finally broken. She hadn't coughed in seven days.

Still Judith sat uncomfortably on her chair beside the bed, her back straight as she could make it, hands pinned between her knees to stop their worrying. "Are you sure it won't return?"

"It . . . feels like it will not," said Hannah. "I think it all ran out of me that morning in Mr. Boott's house."

Judith watched carefully, her face hot, though she knew Hannah was honest: she also still wore her woven ring. Even without it, Judith didn't think Hannah would lie. "Then I wronged you."

"How?"

"You had a precious gift, and now you don't."

"I have much that I treasure more."

"But what will you do without your Sight?"

"Work in the mills," Hannah sighed. "As soon as I can stand without trembling." She folded the covering away from her and leaned forward, to look deeply into Judith's face. "It isn't a bad life for a woman with a union behind her."

"Thanks to you."

"Thanks to you! You turned a key no one's ever turned before. No working woman—nor man either—will have to take just what they're given now."

"The owners won't roll over and let us," Judith warned.

"They'll think of some new strategy."

"Then we must be ever vigilant and teach our sisters," said Hannah, reaching out for her beloved's hand. "Unless you have had enough of Lowell and mills."

"I—"

"Because if you haven't, it isn't a bad life for *two* women. If—if we managed it right, we could have a house of our own one day. Our own den of iniquity and rebellion."

Hannah's hand on hers was warm and urging, but the grip breakable. Judith knew she could break it. Instead, she smoothed the bedclothes and swallowed, and made bold to climb up beside the former Seer. "There's no life I want more."

Acknowledgments

Many people, often without knowing it, enabled the creation of *The Factory Witches of Lowell*. I want to thank:

My workplace family. Paula, Greg, Thinh, J. Hollister, Zara, Ingrid, Bridgette, and the rest of the APL crew.

The real-life organizers I know. Ron, Linda, Karyn, Sarah, Kenny, Patricia, Mike, Rod: you inspire me every day.

My fellow Speculative Wordsmiths, past and present, especially dave ring, who recognizes a love story when he reads one.

The Jellyfish Horde, aka Viable Paradise XXI.

Team Kirby of the 2018 Futurescapes conference: without you, this story would still be languishing on my hard drive.

My sensitivity readers Sam Kassé, Courtni Burleson, and Natasha Lane, for your encouragement and intelligent critiques. Any missteps here are all mine, not theirs.

Carl, my patient and savvy editor, who properly appreciates a flustered capitalist.

Mom and Dad, those oddball Vermonters.

Tay, the (witchy) sister of my heart.

John, who breathes life into me every day.

About the Author

Author photograph by John Musco

C. S. MALERICH grew up in northern New Jersey. In addition to writing, she has taught mythology to undergrads at the University of Maryland and pursued interests in folklore, cultural studies, and public health, sometimes all at once. Her fiction explores intersections of liberation and justice, with an infectious dance beat. Her work has appeared in *Apparition Lit, Ares Magazine,* and the *Among Animals* anthologies. Her novel *Fire & Locket* was published in 2019.

TOR·COM

Science fiction. Fantasy. The universe.

And related subjects.

*

More than just a publisher's website, *Tor.com*

is a venue for **original fiction, comics,** and

discussion of the entire field of SF and fantasy,

in all media and from all sources. Visit our site

today—and join the conversation yourself.